(Vernon Sullivan)

The Dead All Have The Same Skin
(Les morts ont tous la même peau)

with a short story
"Dogs, Desire, and Death" & "Postface"
by Boris Vian

Translated from the French by Paul Knobloch
Introduction by Marc Lapprand

Originally published in French *Les morts ont tous la même peau* by Scorpion in 1947

©Christian Bourgois et Cohérie Boris Vian 1973 et 1998
©Librairie Arthéme Fayard pour l'édition en oeuvres complétes, 1999
©TamTam Books 2007
Translation by Paul Knobloch ©2007
Introduction by Marc Lapprand ©2007
First published by TamTam Books in the U.S.A. 2007
Printed in the United States of America

TamTam Books wants to thank Ichiro Shimizu, Les Zazous, the Boris Vian Estate, Henry Cording, Shirley Berman, Donald Morand, Lun*na Menoh, Bison Ravi, Brian Gottlieb, Prévan, Duke Ellington, Alistair Charles Rolls, le Major, Asuka Hisa, Rachael Small, Kristine McKenna and Kimley Maretzo for their wisdom and assistance on this project.

TamTam Books is edited and published by Tosh Berman.

TamTam Books are art directed and designed by Tom Recchion
With production design by Joseph Shuldiner

tosh@tamtambooks.com
www.tamtambooks.com

First Edition
ISBN 10-digit: 0-9662346-5-0
ISBN 13 digit: 978-0-9662346-5-7
Library of Congress Control Number: 2005911262

The Dead All Have The Same Skin

Boris Vian

(Vernon Sullivan)

The Dead All Have The Same Skin
(Les morts ont tous la même peau)

with a short story
"Dogs, Desire, and Death"
&
"Postface"
by Boris Vian

Translated from the French by Paul Knobloch
Introduction by Marc Lapprand

The Sullivans don't all have the same skin

Here we go again! First of all, under the pseudonym of Vernon
Sullivan, Boris Vian, in 1947, published a French best-sell-
er, *I Spit On Your Graves* (Tamtam Books, 1998). Then, in
the same year, ripe with the swell of success, he also published a second novel: *The Dead All Have The Same Skin*.
This sequel, also published in 1947, is again obsessed with
the question of dubious identities. The hero, Dan Parker, is
a white man living in a world of whites, yet he doubts his
true origin and identity: Is he a real white man or a black
man with white skin? Has he, as they say, crossed the
line? Is Richard his real brother, or is he merely a blackmailer who has detected in Dan the perfect victim to
exploit because of his mysterious identity crisis?

With this second pseudo-hard-boiled thriller signed
by the now famous pen name of Vernon Sullivan, Vian pro-
duces a very convincing psychological and erotic novel. It's
cruder and tighter than the first one, yet not entirely
devoid of humour. But, among the four Sullivan novels, this
one is unique. The first one was a concerted hoax, the
result of a bet between a fledgling publisher, Jean
d'Halluin, and a promising writer, Boris Vian, to produce
the translation of an alleged American novel (*I Spit On
Your Graves*) by an American author who had never exist-
ed (Vernon Sullivan). He wrote it in August of 1946 – in
only two weeks! The last two Sullivans are over-the-top
farces and parodies of the genre. Since the trick is no

longer a secret, Vian/Sullivan makes a point of having a lot of fun, and he clearly exploits this source until the last drop (of ink) has fallen. These two novels will, we hope, also be translated into English.

In his second book, however, Sullivan shines. He perfects his style, and he pushes the limits even further with his main themes, especially Vian's deep-rooted obsessions with both women and literary success. Indeed, the four Sullivans don't seem to have the same skin color at all.

But there's some history behind the novel. In February 1947, a certain Daniel Parker, head of a right-wing organization with the talking name of Cartel d'Action sociale et morale, sued the following people for slander: Vernon Sullivan, author of *I Spit On Your Graves*, Boris Vian, its alleged translator, and Jean d'Halluin, chief-publisher of Éditions du Scorpion. Mr. Parker was already busy with the books of Henry Miller, which he feared were going to pervert French youth with their immoral content; he added Sullivan to the lot. In light of this potent yet unwanted publicity, Boris Vian planned to write a sequel under the same mask: *Les Morts ont tous la même peau*, whose main character, by a strange coincidence, just happens to be called Dan Parker. The book was published in the fall of 1947, but unfortunately its success was limited.

This second thriller centers on the psychological dimension of the protagonist. Being white in a world dominated by whites, Dan, the bouncer at a seedy club in New York, is tired of his violent bouts and pathetic sexual impulses. Yet he constantly fears rejection. He evolves in an environment which he feels will expel him at the first *faux pas*. His insecurity leads him to inexplicably believe that, despite his skin color, he is black. This strange obsession seems to be confirmed by his impotence with white women, including his sexually impatient wife. In fact, the book abounds in erotic scenes. In a progressive and inexorable descent to hell, Dan, the predator of drunk clients and cheap whores, becomes the prey of a con man who claims to be his brother.

Eventually, after he becomes a ruthless serial killer, he finds the police are hot on his heels. Aside from the inevitable racial clichés, the story fascinates because we closely follow Dan's downfall and, unlike him, we realize that he is the agent of his own demise. With just a bit of luck and common sense, he could turn things around, but no one or nothing can save him from doom and his own destruction.

The story unfolds swiftly: no time is wasted on lengthy descriptions or digressions. Action and dialogue build up the novel's momentum. Since Vian has chameleonized that very fashionable pulp genre, he too adopts the same narrative technique, including a different font when the point of view changes. Most of the story is told by Dan himself, with many incursions into his lingering debates. When the narration changes, the font switches from roman to italic characters, and a distance is established between the narrator and Dan, who is then seen from the outside.

Here again, Vian did his homework. Although he never set foot in North-America, he was nevertheless in synch with the latest American production of thrillers and detective novels, which he read either in their French translations or in the original: Katherine-Anne Porter, Erskine Caldwell, Horace Mac Coy, and Carson McCullers were becoming highly fashionable on the French literary scene, and Boris Vian was among their most avid readers.

The novel is followed by a short story which was also included in the original Scorpion edition of 1947: *Les Chiens, le désir et la mort.* Its presence is simply due to the publisher's request to add several pages to the volume. Vian picked this title because its topic is relevant to Sullivan's production. The story also takes place in New York City. It too is full of erotic tension, and it also climaxes with death in a rather gruesome marriage of Eros and Thanatos. On the top of the first page of his manuscript, Vian initially gave it an ominous English title: *They begin with dogs.*

*   *   *

Boris Vian (1920-1959) is unique among twentieth-century French writers. Born into a typically bourgeois yet unconventional family, Vian soon developed eccentric tastes and musical abilities. A memorable concert by Duke Ellington and his band before the war changed him, influencing not only his writings, but also his life-style.

At a very early age, he was diagnosed with a heart murmur that would likely shorten his life. As a result, he approached it with a dazzling intensity. Gilbert Pestureau, one of his most insightful critics, compared his brilliant and short career to the passage of a meteorite. Indeed, one marvels at the amount he wrote in less than twenty years. These collected works were recently published and annotated for the first time in a complete set made up of 15 volumes (Paris, Fayard, 1999-2003). But what makes Vian truly unique on the French literary scene is that he is the epitome of the versatile artist. Trained as an engineer, he only took up that profession for a few years, then started living off his pen after the war. He also played the trumpet in various jazz-bands, and he wrote jazz critiques and monthly chronicles for almost fifteen years. He also wrote fiction, poetry, songs, drama, sketches, libretti, music, articles, speeches, satirical pamphlets, film-scripts and even cocktail recipes (some of which may be found in his *Manual of St-Germain-des-Prés*, Tamtam and Rizzoli Books, 2005).

In his life-time, Vian's reputation was always tinged by scandal; he was known as a writer only by a handful. Today, he is celebrated as an important author, and I do hope that the wonderful work of Tamtam Books will make him known in North America as a fascinating, imaginative writer, capable of instilling in everyday life a certain poetry, a man full of humor and tenderness, as well as irony and, in turns, provocation.

Boris Vian originally prefaced *I Spit On Your Graves* in order to authenticate the existence of Vernon Sullivan, but also to explain why this writer could not be published in the US: Sullivan did not hesitate about leaving his manuscript in France, all the more so as his American publishers had just shown him the timidity of any attempt to publication in his country. Incidentally, it allowed him to justify his courageous position as a translator. The original Scorpion volume of his second novel ended with a *postface* that was in fact intended as a preface. Surprisingly though, Vian does not even mention this second novel. Yet he accomplishes at least two things in it. First, he takes the opportunity to reiterate his real anger about a superficial form of criticism which prevailed in the press, and second, above all, he reaffirms his role as a translator. The idea is that, after reading this short preface, no one is supposed to doubt Sullivan's existence any longer. Vian is merely the translator, and he claims no glory or complicity in the process. He simply asserts that he did the job as requested, but argues that, as a matter of fact, most journalists were only dealing with the alleged forgery regarding *I Spit On Your Graves*. Blinded by what looked like a hoax, they had simply forgotten to actually read the book and talk about it as they should: "When do you plan to start doing your job? When will you stop looking for yourselves in the books you read? A true reader deals with the book itself."

Now, dear reader, thanks to Paul Knobloch and Tosh Berman, it's up to you to start reading this book translated into English for the first time ever, and decide for yourself.

– Marc Lapprand

Preface to *I Spit On Your Graves*. Los Angeles, Tamtam Books, 1998, p. xi.

BORIS VIAN

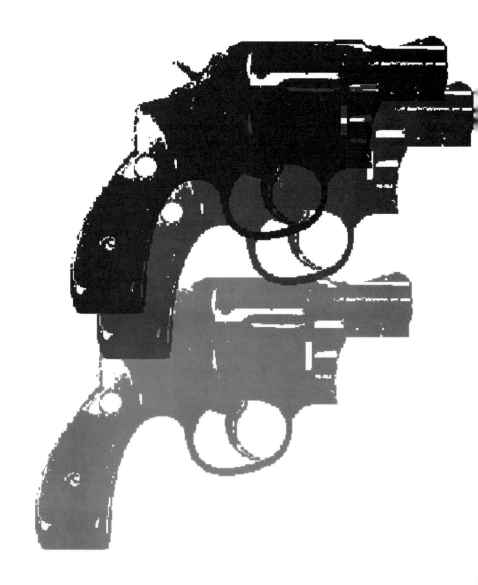

I

We didn't have many customers this evening, and the band was playing a bit sluggishly, as is always the case on nights like these. It was all the same to me. The fewer people the better. Having to toss out half a dozen guys a night, in a more or less orderly fashion to boot, well, in the long run it can end up being a real drag. In the beginning, I liked it.

I liked it. I got a kick out of pummeling the heads of these pigs. But after five years I've started to lose my taste for this particular sport. Five years and not a soul suspects it. No one has the slightest idea that a man of mixed blood, a colored man, has been the one pounding on their heads each and every night. Yeah, in the beginning I really got a charge out of it. And the women. Filthy broads tanked up on whiskey. I'd just shove them into their cars with all their gear and their bellies full of booze. Every night. Every week. Five years.

Nick paid me well for this little job, all because I kept myself presentable and knew how to bring a man to heel without making a scene or causing any fuss. All for a hundred bucks a week.

Most of the people, upstairs and down, kept quiet and minded their own business. A couple in the corner was getting a little loud, but it was nothing serious. Behind the counter Jim was catching a little shuteye.

Upstairs in Nick's room a bunch of riff-raff was busy gambling. Girls were also available if one was so inclined. Still, not just anybody could stroll up.

The two in the corner, some skinny guy and a tired blond got up to dance. They were the only two, so there wasn't much to worry about. The problem was they were getting pretty bruised up smashing into the tables, so I gently escorted them back to their seats.

I stretched out my limbs. Jim was still on the nod and the three musicians were just laying back. Unconsciously, I ran my hand over the lapel of my tuxedo.

The thing is that there was simply no more thrill in dishing out beatings. I had gotten used to it. I was white.

I shuddered inside as I realized what I had just said to myself.

"Pass me a glass, Jim."

"Whiskey?" slurred Jim as he woke from his dream.

"Whiskey."

I was white. I had married a white woman. I had a white child. My mother's father worked as a longshoreman in Saint Louis. A dockworker as black as coal. All my life I'd hated whites. I'd hid and fled from them. I might have resembled them, but back then I also feared them. And now, I can't even understand why I felt what I felt, because I no longer look at the world through the eyes of a Black man. I had been unaware of the slow evolution that had taken place, and now tonight, I found myself changed, transformed, assimilated.

"If they'd only leave..." I said to Jim.

"Yeah," replied Jim, in a weary tone.

I spoke simply because I had to do something. I just had to hear my voice.

"It's too early."

"What does it matter?" I said. "We could close early just this once. Are there a lot of people upstairs?"

"I haven't been able to keep track," said Jim. "Some of them go up that side, and then others take the back way."

The man and the woman were back out on the dance floor. They got tangled up in a chair and came crashing down, causing quite a racket. The woman took a seat, holding her nose in her hand. Her hair was all mussed and she was completely loaded. The man was just sitting where he landed, laughing his ass off.

"Get rid of them," said Jim. "Kick 'em the hell out."

"Whatever," I murmured. "There'll be more where they came from."

I approached the couple and helped the woman up. As for the guy, I grabbed him under the armpits and straightened him out. He wasn't heavy — just another armchair athlete.

"Thanks, sweetheart," he said to me.

The woman started to cry.

"Don't call him sweetheart!" she said. "I'm sweetheart."

"Wouldn't you two like to head back home now?" I proposed.

"No," said the man. "I mean yeah."

"I'll show you to your car," I said. "What color is it?"

"Oh... It's there..." the man indicated by waving his arms through the air in an uncertain gesture.

"Perfect," I said. "Now let's go find it. Come along children."

The woman grabbed hold of my arm.

"Hey! You're strong," she said.

"I'm stronger than him," said the man.

Before I had time to predict his next move he'd belted me one in the stomach. The imbecile didn't have an ounce of muscle on him but he'd still knocked the wind out of me.

"Let's go, let's go," I said.

I had hold of each of them by the arm, and I gave a good squeeze to the man's. He started to turn green.

"Come on," I continued. "We're gonna go home nice and sensible like."

"I don't want to be sensible," said the man.

"Let's go," I repeated. "You know this wouldn't be the first time I've broken a man's arm with this grip of mine."

I dragged him to the door and knocked it open with my foot.

"Which car?" I said.

"The third one..." said the woman. "There..."

With just about the same precision her husband had shown earlier, the woman pointed to one of the cars in the lot. I just counted three down from the first one I saw and pushed them inside.

"Who's driving?" I asked.

"She is," said the man.

I'd guessed right. I closed the door behind them.

"Sweet dreams," I beckoned.

"Bye bye," waved the man.

I went back to the bar. Nothing had changed. A couple of customers got up to leave. I yawned. Jim yawned.

"What a way to make a living," he sighed.

"Hurry on down, Nick..." I said.

Nick's descent always signaled closing time.

"Hurry on down..." echoed Jim.

I talked like him. I was like him. He didn't even look at me when we spoke, which was all the more proof.

Then, from under the bar, I heard the buzzer ring twice. They needed me upstairs.

"Go on," said Jim. "Kick 'em all out."

I pushed back the velvet curtain that concealed the staircase and crawled up past the last step, swearing to myself all the way. For Christ's sake, I wish these sons of bitches would just leave me be and let me go home in peace.

My wife is surely asleep by now... in a warm and comforting bed.

II

Dull thuds rang out as my feet pounded over the metal and concrete staircase. I made my way up with supple steadiness. I never ignored an opportunity to exercise these sacred muscles of mine. I owed them at least that much. At the end of the staircase there was another velvet curtain. Nick really liked velvet. Velvet and fat women. And money...

The room on the second floor had a low ceiling and the sides were decorated with deep red wallpaper. A couple dozen guys were busy losing their dough under the spell of Nick's handsome eyes. Along one of the walls, Nick had set up four little cubicles with tables where the more ardent clientele could avail themselves of the soothing comforts of the club's regular girls. I don't know if Nick hit them up for a percentage, or vice-versa, but there was always plenty of work and the girls were constantly busy sorting things out with the boss.

I was once again summoned upstairs to resolve a dispute brewing in one of these little cubicles, which as far as I was concerned were more trouble than they were worth. When I entered the room there were five of them hunched over the entrance to one of the little booths. When Nick saw me he signaled that it was time to put an end to their quiet little séance. Two of the girls tried to drag a couple of them away by their shirtsleeves, but to no avail. Things started to turn sour when I grabbed the first guy by the shoulder. The blow that was unquestionably headed my way had instead struck Maxine, a cute little blonde, right in the kisser. I couldn't help but grin when I saw the look on her face. The guy was too wasted to have struck her very hard, but just a moment ago she had given him the blow-off, and now she was more than a little pissed off.

"You pig bastard!"

Her voice was like the sting of a moray eel. And she didn't stop there. She proceeded to give him a good slapping around — the kind that a guy doesn't take lightly, even if that guy happens to be a drunk. I was still right behind him. Just when he was about ready to give her the payback, I grabbed his arm and turned things to my advantage. I tried not to be too underhanded about it, mind you, for in all honesty, I could understand how he felt.

While all this was happening I decided to size things up around me. The two in the cubicle would surely be ready to go all out. The girl's blouse was hiked up just over her tits and one could see right away that her father was surely an Irishman, given the plentitude of freckles and her pretty blue eyes. The guy was lying on top of her, slobbering over her belly. He must have been a good customer because the two of them had trashed up the little box like it was nobody's business.

They were literally swimming in whiskey. The man was a little better off than the girl, but only because he happened to be resting on top of her.

I took the guy and sent him flying into the wall. He just stuck there. It looked to me like his arm was bothering him a bit. Anyway, he tried to use the other one to prop himself up, but he had absolutely no force left. The four others, apparently, hadn't noticed a thing, and Nick, who was hip to how things worked, signaled to Maxine to keep her mouth shut.

I walked up to the ringleader of the little quartet and let my words fly right in his face:

"Would you fellows mind heading home now?"

He didn't move a muscle. I turned around and Nick gave me the look. That was that. Time to play hardball.

"Get the fuck out of here! All four of you."

Right as I said it I grabbed two of them by the arms and shoved them towards the staircase. Nick, who is no fool when it comes to using his fists, took care of seeing them down. Anyway, even a half-unconscious idiot can make his way down a staircase without too much danger. Legs function on reflex, I think. Either that or these people are used to being cracked on the skull.

I sent the other two over to Nick. The gamblers kept at their game like nothing had happened. Nick's clientele would all of a sudden get really well behaved when I started to use my muscle. Very discrete. It was just these two cretins over in the cubicle who insisted on continuing with their over-the-top burlesque show.

O.K. Now for them.

I strode right into the little box. The man hardly moved. I grabbed him, sat him up in the chair, and buttoned up his jacket. I had to. I wanted to do the same for the girl, but this proved tricky. As soon as she felt my hands on her she started squirming like a worm, got tangled up in my legs, and pulled me down on top of her. She was a real piece of work. We didn't see her that often at Nick's, but she came more or less on a regular basis. I can't remember what they called her.

"Come on, let's go." I told her. "Get your head together, babe."

"Oh, nuts!"

She just laughed like mad and was hanging on to me, shaking my body like it was an apple tree. It was hard to resist all this, because after all, I was being treated to a first-class example of exhibitionism. But in the end I succeeded in getting her dress back over her thighs.

"Come along, my pretty. Time to go to bed."

"Yeah! You're right. Take me home."

"It's the gentleman who'll see you back."

"No. Not him... There's nothin' left in that guy. He's

sloshed."

I picked her up and sat her down next to the drunk. But he was like a cadaver. Really.

Nick came over.

"The four others are outside," he said. "Get rid of these two."

"She's still O.K. But the gentleman here, he can't even stand on his own two feet."

"Just bring 'em," said Nick.

I grabbed the guy under his armpits and the girl was hanging onto my shoulder. She stroked my biceps.

"His car's outside. Come on. I'll take you to it."

"Walk on ahead," I told her.

Trying to carry the two of them was no piece of cake. Fortunately, the girl could at least walk, more or less.

I made my way down the staircase and passed through the hallway behind the bar where we exited the building.

"So where's the car?"

She looked around.

"There. The blue one."

No mistake this time. Still, the cool air had no effect on my client. The girl opened the front door.

"Put him in."

I shoved him in as best I could and he fell, sprawled out over the seat.

"He'll never be able to drive you home."

She held on to my arm, squeezing it more tightly.

"What am I going to do?"

"He'll wake up."

I was being optimistic.

"I'm scared. Can't you stay with me? Can't you take me home?"

"How am I supposed to do that?"

"With his car."

I'd really had enough. I wanted to go to sleep. I wanted to get back to my wife. What a job! She was rubbing up against me like a dog in heat.

"Forget it," I said.

"Come on."

She moved into the car and grabbed hold of my arm. She stank of whiskey and perfume, but still, I was just about ready to give in. I was really ready when I saw her turn over on the seat and hike her dress up in one swift movement. This was one chick who didn't need any phony, padded bra.

"Stay there," I said. "We'll go find a quiet little corner."

"Come on... Hurry up. I can't wait."

"You can wait a lousy five minutes."

She let out a light little chuckle so enticing that my hands trembled as I opened the front door. I hit the gas and drove towards Central Park, still the most convenient place. We didn't even close the car doors when we got out. I just took her on the ground, in the first dark corner I could find.

It wasn't very warm, but we were rubbing up against one another so furiously that I could see the vapor rise from her skin in the cool air while her nails dug into the fabric of my jacket. She took no precautions. They never did.

III

So that was that for this particular evening. I drove the guy's car back to Nick's place. The drunk was still on the nod and the broad was not much better off than he was. The stink of the whiskey and the broad was all over me. I left them parked at the entrance. I walked upstairs just to make sure everything was O.K. It was completely quiet. I came back downstairs. Not a soul. I could go back home and sleep now.

Jim let out a yawn as he put on his coat.

"One more boring evening," I said.

"Nothing out of the ordinary," concurred Jim.

"Nothing..." I said.

Nothing. Nothing except that today represented five years. Five years and nobody has caught on. Five years of stomping on these fools' heads and then banging their women. Without thinking I slammed my fist into the wall, but I hit it a bit too hard and stood there shaking my hand and groaning. I had once again let these fools get to me.

I was more white than they were simply because I enjoyed being white now. And so what?

I didn't give a damn. I quite simply couldn't care less. It wasn't so bad being white. Especially with a white woman in your bed and a white kid who'll one day be able to make something of himself.

Why was Jim still yawning?

"Good night," I said.

I pushed my way through the door and stretched out my limbs as I left. The station wasn't far off.

My wife wasn't far off either. My back was a bit sore. She had really dug her nails in. But it was nothing to worry about. I was still in fine form.

There's nothing like New York in springtime.

The subway. Fifteen minutes. More people. My street. My house. Calm and quiet.

The odor of whiskey still clung to my clothing, but worse yet my hands smelled like the woman. A nice smell. The smell of a blue-eyed girl with an Irish father.

I silently made my way up the three flights, always bending the knees, working the muscles. My keys jangled in my pocket. My three keys. I recognized the one I needed by its weightiness and took it out.

The lock opened. Naturally.

I shut the thickly paneled door and without turning on the lights headed to the bathroom. But then I tripped and fell right on top of a body that had been lying in the darkness.

I instantly untangled myself, got up, and flipped on the light switch. The whole room was lit up. I stood there frozen, like I was nailed to the floor. He hadn't even woken up. He was snoring. Drunk, no doubt. That filthy nigger. Richard. He was bone thin and was wearing a soiled suit. And he smelled real bad. I could smell his stink from where I was standing. Inside, my heart was beating irregularly, pounding like the organ of a tormented beast. I didn't dare take a step or make any attempt to move. I couldn't dare risk going to see if Sheila had found out the truth. There was a cupboard behind me. Without taking my eyes off Richard, I fumbled around and found a bottle of rye. I drank... five, six big gulps. But Richard was still lying in front of me, and there was no noise coming from the open door of the bedroom. The world around me was dead and sleeping. I looked at my hands. I touched my face. I looked at Richard and started to laugh. My brother had found me.

His body started to stir and I moved closer to him. I picked him up with one hand. He was half-asleep, and I gave him a good shake.

"Wake up, bastard."

"What's the matter?" he said.

He opened his eyes and saw me. His expression remained unchanged.

"What the fuck are you doing here?"

"I found you, Dan. You see. The Good Lord wanted us to have this reunion."

"Where's Sheila?"

"Who's Sheila?" he said.

"Well, who opened the door?"

"I just came in. There was no one here."

I left him there and ran into the bedroom. Sheila had left a little note on the dresser, in the usual place: "I'm at mom's with the baby. Love and kisses."

I must have bumped into a piece of furniture. My head was still functioning, but not my legs. I walked back slowly into the hall.

"You get the hell outta here!"

"But Dan..."

"Get the hell out. Beat it. I don't know you."

"But Dan, the Good Lord has led me back to you."

"Get the hell out, I said!"

"But I haven't got any money."

"Take this."

I dug into my pocket and handed him a ten-dollar bill. He grabbed it, looked it over and stuck it into his pocket. His dazed look had vanished.

"Don't you understand that it's not too sharp for a nigger to show up at a white man's house?"

"I'm your brother, Dan. I've even got the papers."

I was all over him in nothing flat. I seized him by the back of the neck and spat out a stream of curses and threats.

"So you've got papers, huh? What papers, you bastard!"

"I've got the same name as you, Dan. As the Good Lord says, thou shall not deny thy mother and father."

I did the one thing that I shouldn't have. I tightened my fist and sent it smashing into his lower lip. I felt his teeth crack and a vague feeling of shame came over me. Richard didn't even flinch. But his eyes were fixed on me, and I saw in them... No. I must be crazy. You can't see anything in a person's eyes. There's nothing to see. I tried to remain rational. I tried desperately. But Richard said nothing, and as he looked at me I was overcome with fear.

"Where you working now, Dan?"

The wound I had inflicted altered his speech and a

stream of blood was running down his chin. He wiped at it with the back of his hand.

"Just get the hell out, Richard. And if you value your life at all you'd better never set foot here again."

"But where can I see you, Dan?"

"I have no desire to see you."

"Well maybe Sheila would like to..." he speculated.

Once again, I had to hold back the desire to kill him: a desire that cut through my soul like a razor-sharp blade.

He walked towards the door and delicately touched his shredded lip.

"Get out."

"Ten bucks," he said. "That's not much."

This was my brother. And I wanted him dead. I was in the grips of a hideous anguish that was eating away at my guts. I was afraid he'd come back. I wanted to know.

"Hold on," I said. "Who gave you my address?"

"Oh, no one in particular," he said. "Some friends. I'm going to go now, Dan. I'll see you later. I'll drop by your work."

"You don't know where I work."

"That doesn't matter, Dan. It really doesn't matter."

"How did you get the door open?"

"I open doors, Dan. Yes, the good lord can surely attest to the fact that I am an opener of doors. I'll see you Dan. I'll see you real soon."

I watched, dumbfounded, as he left. His skin was coal black and he smelled like a nigger. Hell, he was a nigger.

My watch showed five-thirty in the morning. Day was beginning to dawn. Dairymen outside. Sheila had slept at her mother's with the baby.

I closed the door to the apartment and started to undress. I didn't know what I was doing. I took a look around and then headed toward the bedroom and stopped just before

BORIS VIAN

entering. I changed my mind and headed towards the bathroom. I stood in front of the mirror. Looking back at me was a solidly built man of about thirty-five years of age, large and well proportioned. I had nothing to say to him. He was white. No doubt about it. But I didn't like the expression in his eyes...

...the eyes of someone who had just seen a ghost.

IV

After that day I started searching for a new apartment, but it was really difficult. I would have to drop a big chunk of dough. I didn't talk to Sheila about it. I knew she really liked the place we had and I was afraid to tell her. What possible reason could I give her? In the street, I was constantly turning around to see if someone was following me. I was on the lookout for Richard's skinny silhouette, the shade of his mulatto skin, his rumpled suit and his long arms. The memories that remained from my childhood, those concerning Richard, were all of a troubling and disquieting nature, although I could not determine just when they became troublesome, for after all, they were simply common childhood memories. Richard was the darkest of the three of us, and undoubtedly, that fact in and of itself at least partially explained my uneasiness.

I made my way to Nick's through a series of detours, getting off one station ahead of or one station after my usual stop, and then, in order to get to the bar, I followed a complex little path, a kind of labyrinth that I pleasurably wove into the neighboring streets. This exhausting game – mentally exhausting I mean - nevertheless brought me a false sense of security which created a deceptively comforting little cage that protected me from blindsided attacks.

Of course, I would sooner or later have to walk through that door at Nick's, without seeming too cautious or looking over my shoulder. And that's just exactly what I did, no different from any other day.

Jim was distractedly leafing through the evening paper that was spread out behind the counter. His eyes moved up to meet mine as I entered.

"Hey," he said.

"Hey."

"Some guy came by to see you."

I stopped dead in my tracks. Then, remembering that we had customers, I passed behind the counter and headed toward the dressing room to change my clothes.

"What guy?"

"I don't know. He just wanted to see you."

"Why?"

"Dunno."

"Just a regular guy?"

"Yeah, just a regular guy. What's going on with you?"

"Nothing."

"Oh... O.K."

He returned to his reading and then popped his head back up to add something else.

"He's coming back in an hour."

"Here?"

"Of course. I told him you'd be here."

"Alright."

"Something wrong with that?"

There wasn't a hint of interest in his voice. Just curiosity, pure and simple.

"Why should there be anything wrong? I don't even know the guy."

"You weren't expecting someone?"

"Expecting someone?"

"Oh...." sighed Jim.

I went into the dressing room and started to change. One hour. It surely wasn't Richard. Jim would have told me if the guy were black.

So who could it be?

I'd simply have to wait for an hour. I finished getting ready and came back to the bar.

"Give me whiskey and water, Jim."

"Easy on the whiskey?" asked Jim.

"Easy on the water."

He remained quiet and looked at me as he filled my glass. I drank down the cool and harsh liquid in one gulp and then asked for another. I didn't really like alcohol. I felt it bite into my stomach, but I remained calm — perfectly calm and braced.

I sat at the end of the bar, in a spot where I could easily check out the clientele as they came and went.

I waited.

Two girls came in. Regulars. They smiled at me. As they walked by I gently passed my hand over their asses, whose well-worked shapes were accentuated by their tight-fitting outfits. They sat down at a table not far from the bar. Good clients. With girls like those it was easy for Nick to make his afternoon cut.

I had a good time just looking at them. Nice make-up. Clean. A couple of real dishes. Two beautiful, blonde machines. I was thinking about Richard so intensely that I made a defensive movement. I tried to cover it up by prolonging it into a somewhat larger gesture.

While Jim was working his cash register I suddenly realized that he was staring at me rather strangely. As soon as he saw me looking back he turned away.

It was horrific to just sit here and wait. I tried to distract myself. I stared at the ground and the walls and the ceiling and the luminescent tubes in the lighting fixtures. I stared at the bottles neatly tucked away in nooks and crannies of chrome, and at the new clients and the regulars. From where I was perched, up high on a barstool, I couldn't really dive into the thighs of the little brunette. I got off my stool and pulled up a chair directly opposite her. She knew exactly what I was up to and obliged me by spreading her legs just a bit more so that I could get a gander. There wasn't really enough light, but nothing was blocking my view, and what I saw looked pleasant and comforting.

She gave me a signal and then headed off to the restrooms. I got up.

Maybe this would be a good way to kill some time before that guy got here.

I took a slightly different route than her, disappearing behind the staircase that led to the game room. Behind the velvet curtain we caught up to each other and headed down the hall, where we could make our descent on down to the restrooms on the other side.

One of Nick's little work projects was to transform the telephone booths into comfortable little play stations. Sure, they were a little cramped, but in general no one complained.

She was waiting for me in the first booth. She knew what I wanted.

I also knew and I headed straight in. She was in there, casually smoking, which bothered me a bit. She hadn't come for the sole purpose of rendering me service, but there are always ways to get them stirred up and ready for action.

Right then and there she dropped her cigarette and planted her lips on mine. I gently nibbled on her tender and perfumed flesh. I was happy. A big white circle of well-being enveloped me, like a cloud of cotton. Her curvy, silky skin moved forward in search of my hand and she quickly found it as the two of us stood in the booth. She closed her eyes and shivered a bit, and then, without breaking our embrace, she calmed down and lit another cigarette. I grabbed her backside and ran my hands over the curves and arches of her body. I felt good.

We separated without saying a word and I got myself nicely cleaned up. She opened her purse and took out her lipstick. I quietly shut the door to the booth and made my way back to the stairs.

I climbed up rather speedily. The anguish, which had for a moment dissipated, had now come back and seized me for a third time.

Jim hadn't moved from his spot. Nobody new had come in. I keenly scanned past the bar and through the tables.

"Give me a whiskey, Jim."

He served me. I drank it and set down the glass. And then I froze. A guy walked through the door. One single, normal, ordinary guy.

Jim raised his chin, pointing him out to me.

"There's your customer."

"Right," I said.

I remained seated.

Not seeming to recognize me, he headed over to Jim.

"Dan here?"

"That's him," said Jim, pointing me out.

"Hello," said the guy.

He looked at me attentively.

"Can I buy you a drink?"

"Whiskey," I said.

He ordered two whiskeys. He wasn't too tall, but he was massively built.

"So you wanted to see me?"

"Yeah," he said. "It's about your brother, Richard."

"You one of his friends?"

"No," said the guy. "I don't make friends with niggers."

He was looking for some reaction from me as he spoke those words. I didn't even flinch.

"Neither do I," I told him.

"Is Richard really your brother?"

"We've got different fathers."

"So it was his father who was black?"

I didn't respond. He was waiting, sipping slowly at his whiskey. Jim was at the other end of the counter.

"Come on," I said to him. "Let's go find a quiet little corner."

I grabbed our glasses and moved towards one of the tables. Just then the little brunette who I'd jumped came walking out of the restroom. As she sat down she shot me a smile and I responded with an almost unconscious little wink.

We sat down.

"Go ahead," I said. "Let me have it."

"Richard's not allowed in here," he said. "So he gave me fifty bucks and I came for him."

"Fifty bucks? Just where would he get his hands on fifty bucks?"

"He'll take it out of the hundred that you're going to give me for him."

I was breathing heavily. I held on to the edge of the table with my two hands and saw my knuckles start to turn white.

"And what if I don't have a hundred dollars?"

"Well then the boss of this joint just might be interested in knowing about the color of your brother's skin."

"Nick? He wouldn't give a flying fuck," I assured him.

The man seemed disconcerted. He looked at me. Sure he could look at me. Plenty of others had also had the time to look me over during these last five years.

"So how do you know Richard?" I asked.

"Met him in a bar."

"You're mulatto," I suddenly shouted out. "Let me see your fingernails."

He got up.

"I'm sorry," he said. "But I'm going to absolutely have to get that hundred dollars. If not, I'll have to ask someone else, maybe even someone you know."

I also stood up. I was poorly positioned, with not much room to maneuver, but I could really feel the force of the blow in my left arm as it retracted. His jaw cracked, and I moved over to his right and grabbed him by the collar of his suit just as he was gently falling to the ground.

I opened and closed my left hand two or three times. I felt good. A girl and a fight. That's life. Where did I get the idea that it could ever be anything else? Jesus Christ! If I just had the time to wipe them all out, annihilate them all before they ruin my life, I swear to God that afterwards, there'd be no more gloomy days in this boy's life.

Of course, nobody had noticed our little fisticuffs.

Jim was looking at me. He turned away as soon as our eyes met. The guy had managed to stagger back to his feet. I don't know how he was able to hold himself up. He was probably completely unconscious, but standing. I sat him in a chair and waited. He seemed to be making an effort to open his eyelids and then he executed a big, long swallow. His hand wandered towards my chin as if it were searching out some precious object.

"Get up," I said.

"Why?" he murmured.

"We're going to see Richard."

"No."

I tightened my fist and casually started tapping at the edge of the table.

"I don't know where he is," he added.

"When were you supposed to see him?"

"Tonight."

"Then it's time. Come on, I'll follow you."

"I'm thirsty," he said.

"Drink your whiskey. There's still some left."

He had a hard time gulping it down. He looked really tired.

"I don't know where Richard is," he repeated.

Even he didn't seem convinced of what he was saying.

"Neither do I. That's exactly why we have to go and find him. Come on."

I got up and then grabbed him and walked over to the bar.

"Jim," I said. "Could you lend me your coat?"

Jim headed towards the dressing room.

"So," I continued, "just where is our good friend Richard?"

I suddenly noticed my face in the mirror behind the bar and I understood why the guy wasn't talking back. I was, nevertheless, calm, at least much more so than the night when I found Richard sleeping in my hallway.

I was either going to finish cleaning up this mess tonight or simply abandon everything. Everything. The girls and the booths and Sheila and the kid. All of a sudden it all really mattered to me. That, and the whiskey, and smashing in the faces of those nitwits who don't even dare to try and make love without a belly full of booze.

Jim handed me his raincoat and I put it on because I didn't want to head out into the streets dressed as I was.

"Get going," I said to the guy.

Nick wouldn't ask any questions. This type of thing didn't happen often.

The guy walked out in front of me.

"Is it far?" I asked.

"Not too far," he said. "Around 115th street. Harlem."

"Is this something you do a lot of? Working out cons and hustles with a bunch of filthy niggers?"

"It can be profitable," he said.

"That's the kind of thing every average Joe should tell himself," I reflected. "But those kinds of thoughts seem to get the average Joe a little too excited."

He looked at me. He was worried. I was a lot bigger than him, but he was pretty hefty. He was built like a beer barrel.

"You enjoy this kind of thing?" I asked. "Getting your ass kicked?"

"For fifty dollars," he said, "I can live with it."

"I'd really like to know what fifty dollars you're talking about," I jested. "Unless my self-proclaimed brother Richard has found another sucker in the meantime."

"Why are you coming if he's not your brother?" said the man.

"I just like to see their mugs," I said.

I understood the spot I was in. I was caught between two places, at the halfway point, and I realized that sooner or later I'd have to choose. The day had come. I thought about Sheila, the telephone booth, the blows on the head that those niggers got during the riot in Detroit, and I laughed out loud, sarcastically. It's easy to choose whether you want to give those blows or get them. Myself, I preferred giving them.

Even if that meant giving a few to my splendid bastard of a brother Richard.

I hailed a passing taxi and gave the address to the driver.

V

It was dirty inside and the place stank. The guy with me said a few words to the nigger behind the bar who pointed us towards the staircase that led to the basement. Without turning around, I climbed down the first step. I don't know if there were a lot of customers; it would have been impossible for me to try and describe this little bistro, which from just a quick glance looked like all the others.

It was hard to understand the layout of the joint. At the bottom of the stairs there was a hallway that turned at a right angle. We followed it to the end, where I saw a second staircase that led upstairs. It would have been easy to confuse the two. Finally we stopped at the third door.

Inside the filthy, smoke-filled room were a couple of coffee-colored girls and a man. One of them was sitting at a table waiting for God knows what, just doing nothing. As for the man and the other chick, they were busy fooling around on a shabby old sofa, thoroughly unembarrassed by our presence. The girl had taken off her dress and what remained of her undergarments did little to cover up what should have been covered.

The man, of course, was Richard. His emaciated face was glowing with sweat as he slowly caressed his companion's thighs. The two of them were stretched out along the sofa and I saw Richard's hands make their way up towards the two firm globes that were shoved into a grimy bra whose resistance was being pushed to the most extreme of limits.

It was a good idea to have had that little tumble with the brunette back at Nick's because this little scene really disgusted me. Still, I've got to admit that despite the disgust, something was stirring in me. The room was a mess. It reeked of sweat. A shiver ran through me, yet it wasn't really unpleasant.

None of the three bothered getting up when they saw me come in. All you could hear was the panting of the woman on the couch and Richard moving around. His eyes were closed.

I was surprised to find myself staring at the other girl. Her hair was long and straight and she had a rather prominent mouth and long, fine hands. Unfortunately, the guy broke the charm of the moment when he interrupted.

"Richard," he blurted out, "it's your brother."

Richard slowly opened his eyes. He propped himself up on one elbow, the girl still in his arms. With his hand, he tugged at her bra, which all of a sudden snapped open. Her circular, brown nipples, which were quite ample, contrasted with the lighter color of her skin, and I saw Richard's fingers grip into the elastic flesh that was offered up to him.

"Hey, Dan," he said.

I didn't respond.

"I figured that you'd come," he said. "Brothers can't abandon one another."

"I'm not your brother," I told him. "And you know it."

Without a trace of emotion he shoved the girl on the sofa out of his way and moved right over her. He seemed to be lightheaded, like he was high on something. He must have smoked some marijuana or some other crap like that.

"But sure you are," he said.

The girl barely moved. She leaned her head to the side and folded her arms up around her face. I saw the glowing drops of sweat underneath her armpits. Somehow my wrath had seemed to vanish and I felt tired. Sort of weary, but still nervous. The other girl just sat at the table, tapping at it with her long, bony fingers.

The guy just stared at us and then he shrugged his shoulders and left. I could hear him make his way up and down the lengths of the hallway.

The girl on the bed was letting out little moans of pleasure, but Richard broke loose from her and stood up. He straightened out his clothes and sat down at the table. The girl, still unsatisfied, wanted more, and her chest and hips stirred under the soiled sheets.

"What do you want?" I said to Richard.

All of a sudden he seemed to me so harmless that I could scarcely recall the terror and emotion which had gripped me the day I'd found him at my place. I stood there asking myself why I had bothered looking for a new apartment. For this skinny, worn-out little mulatto? For this guy so distant from me?

"How about a hundred dollars?" asked Richard. "I'm busted."

"I don't have a hundred."

"You know it's your duty to help your brother," said Richard. "The Good Lord wanted me to find you. You and my sister Sheila."

My eyes moved up quickly and I saw the look on his face. Shifty and inquisitive, with a vague smile on his lips, he slyly sized me up. He passed his hand over his sweaty forehead and then turned away and looked at something over in the corner of the room.

In all my confusion, I started to feel that I was putting myself at risk, like the other day. But I was unable to react. There was an instant of hesitation. For a moment, I asked myself if blood was stronger than reason, and if this black blood of mine wasn't pulling me inexorably toward Richard, in spite of all those years of reflexes acquired in the presence of Whites. But that was ridiculous. Impossible. I was firmly hooked into the White world and I could feel those hooks in my flesh, in my habits, and even in the familiar manner in which I was treated. I especially felt a sense of "being at home" whenever I was around them. I was also hooked because of Sheila, and because of my son, who would get a good education, go to college, and be somebody - somebody wealthy and respected, with black servants and a private plane.

"Listen, Richard. Let's say I give you a hundred bucks. Will you promise to go back to Chicago and leave me be?"

"With God as my witness," said Richard as he stood back up. "But I won't survive too long on just a hundred bucks."

"I'll send you some money every month."

The words were hard to swallow. Why don't I just stomp him out right now? Why not just get rid of him? I could no longer make any sense of my feelings. I felt like I was at the edge of an abyss. The smallest little fracture in the rhythm of time and all equilibrium would vanish.

"How much?" said Richard.

The girl on the couch remained motionless. Her shiny eyes were fixed upon us and she shot me a glance.

Footsteps. Dull thuds making their way down the hall.

"I'll send you some money," I repeated.

The words were tough to swallow. I wanted to think about something else. I had to think about something else.

"I have to give fifty to my friend," said Richard. "After that, there's not much left for me."

"Go get him."

He stepped out and brought the guy back in.

"You're gonna get lost now," I said to the guy.

"O.K.," he replied. "No reason to get nasty."

I really didn't want to hurt him, but I gave him a blow that sent him rolling a couple of yards.

"Get up," I told him.

The girls kept quiet and I could hear their heavy and labored breathing.

"You're gonna hit the road with this twenty bucks," I said, pulling the bills from my pocket. "And if I ever see your face again you won't even be able to recognize yourself after I get through with you."

"Hand it over," he said. "I don't expect to ever see you again. That goes for the both of you."

He crammed the bills into his pocket and left. I could hear his footsteps on the staircase, then nothing.

The girl on the sofa got up, completely nude, and closed the door. She walked over to Richard and sat down at the table. I could smell her hot, pungent odor. She looked over at me and let out a vague laugh.

What was I going to do with him? Am I going to have to kill Richard? I looked at the bodies of the two girls and at my skinny brother and his shifty eyes. The frightful odor invaded my head, sending shivers up and down my spine. I imagined my hands throttled around his stiff, wiry neck... the girls screaming... Of course I was going to have to get rid of him, and in a way that wouldn't involve paying him off and sending him back to Chicago. Of course. But I'd also have to get rid of the two girls as well. There was no way around it. It was just something that had to be done.

"Go get some whiskey," I said to the one who still had some clothes on. "What's your name?"

"Anne," she said.

"I'm Sally," added the other.

With her head resting on her shoulder she proceeded to gaze at me, rather deviously. Her round thighs were flattened out over the scratched up surface of the table and beads of sweat rolled down from her armpits onto her firm waistline. She casually shifted her position. I could now see her naked underbelly, scarcely covered by a piece of down fabric slightly darker than her flesh. Closing my eyes, I imagined the abundant mass of her cunt thrusting itself into my hands, and I felt myself slipping, losing control of the game. I made an effort to get back on the ball. I tried to reflect on Sheila, on my son, and how this might utterly ruin everything and bring an end to all my dreams. But did Richard, with his skinny little neck and grimy hands, really represent any danger for me? The smell of these two women, these Blacks, now somehow seemed muted. It came from everywhere. It came from the old, chipped paint on the dirty walls, from the cold, damp floor, and from the ancient sofa. It came from the table and from the legs of this girl. It came from her chest, which I now saw tighten with impatience. It came from her thighs, and that hard, hot little triangle that I was now going to pounce upon with all my force.

Richard stretched out and rested his elbows on the table. Sally stared at him, full of sweetness, and ran her fingers through his hair. They were long, agile fingers, and I thought about them running all over my body. I had given Anne five dollars and she had left to go and get a bottle of whiskey. I was going to have a few drinks of whiskey. Once again Richard's cold, hard eyes met mine. He wasn't waiting for any whiskey. Money was all he was after.

My emotional state alternated between fear and forgetful oblivion. The sexual excitement that had swept me away was making it difficult to concentrate on the possible consequences of Richard's presence, which for days had been my only obsession. I was no longer thinking. There were just lightening bolts of images flashing through my head. I repeatedly saw two bodies lying on the sofa: Sally's and mine. Richard was keeping a close eye on me.

I moved over to the table. Just a simple look and Sally would be mine.

But it was Sally who made the first move. She stood up, pressed her body against mine, and took hold of my right hand, which she guided onto her pointed breasts. Richard didn't move a muscle. I heard the door open. Anne entered, locked the door behind her and set the bottle on the table. Richard snatched it up, hesitated, and finally opened it and started greedily guzzling down the booze as I looked on.

Anne smiled at me when our eyes met. She was waiting for her hit on the bottle. I could feel Sally stir and squirm, and I knew I had better keep my attention on her. She abruptly broke loose from our embrace and helped me take off my raincoat. I tossed my hat to the side.

Richard had stopped drinking. He passed the bottle to Anne. Anne took a hit and then it was my turn. While I drank, the two girls removed the rest of my clothes. Richard had passed out, his head resting on his elbows. I took Sally over to the sofa. She had the bottle and when she passed it back to me it was empty. My lips caressed the surface of her skin, the bitter moisture of her sweat, and I wanted to sink my teeth right into her flesh. She pulled me towards her, guiding my head, and I could feel her offering herself up to me as I kissed her. All the while, I could also feel Anne sliding up against me. I took her brutally, so much so that I expected her to scream out. We were three naked, smoking bodies in the middle of a cold room, and I had utterly forgotten about my white skin.

VI

My arms and legs ached and my head pounded mercilessly as I attempted to break free from their tangled bodies. Sally's head just flopped back, inert. I tried to prop her up on the divan but she simply lapsed into oblivion again. She smiled vaguely and tried to open her eyes, but they fell closed. Anne shook her body around like a dog coming out of the water and I was overcome by its elastic grace: a model's body, long and thin, with firm little high breasts and fragile, delicate bones. She moved with the supple finesse of a wild animal. Sheila often moved this same way when she was lounging about.

Sheila. I looked at the time. Jim must be getting suspicious. And Nick? No, Nick wouldn't say anything. I stared at the table, seized by a sudden fear. My clothes were over on the table and Richard was asleep, his head resting in his folded arms.

I didn't have any hundred dollars on me. I would have to come back. Why not take advantage of Richard's deep little slumber?

I got up and moved around a bit. I was feeling just fine. That foggy confusion had suddenly disappeared. Two girls at once. Certainly the best cure for too much whiskey. Sally's mouth hung open as she lay resting. I smelled my hands. A feeling of disgust seized me. My entire body was now impregnated with their odor. I was shaking, but then I saw the ochre-colored body of the second girl who was getting dressed, and she was so carefree as she hummed a little ditty that I found myself wanting her again. I could feel her flesh around mine, smothering and fiery. But I couldn't keep myself from thinking of Sheila's face, her wavy, blonde hair, her scarlet lips, and the blue-veined flesh of her naked breasts.

I didn't want to give that hundred dollars to Richard. He was sleeping. All I had to do was leave.

I grabbed my clothes and quickly got dressed. I would have liked to take a shower, but I had to hurry. I had to get back to Nick's, back to my duties. I was lucky that this had happened during the afternoon. Generally speaking, I never had much to do in the afternoon.

How am I going to be able to get rid of this smell? I was sure that Sheila would notice it. As I started to understand the implications of my situation, I could feel my senses start to take hold again and my mind bore the marks of all these new, violent impressions.

Richard remained motionless, in deep sleep. I was now lucid. Too lucid. I hadn't moved an inch. I had let myself get carried away by desire. All white men — men like me — want to sleep with blacks. It's not just a question of race. It's a natural reflex. We imagine it will be different.

It is.

Disconcerted, I tightened my fists. I walked round in circles. Anne was watching me, malicious and satisfied.

"So when are you coming back?" she murmured.

"I'm not coming back," I said brutally.

"Don't you want to see Richard?"

She moved over to him, wanting to wake him, no doubt.

"Don't touch him," I said curtly.

She stood still and obedient.

"Why don't you want to come back?" she asked.

"I'm not his brother. And I'm none too fond of his skin color, either. I have no plans to see him again."

"You like my color?" she smiled.

There wasn't one inch of her skin that hadn't been in intimate contact with mine, and I could remember each inch with precise detail.

"I'm a White man," I said. "There can't be anything between us."

She shrugged her shoulders.

"A lot of Whites live with Blacks. We're not in the south, you know. This is New York."

"I don't need you. I'm happy as I am. I don't have any intention of being exploited by a bunch of niggers."

She stood there smiling and I started to swell with anger.

"I can get by without the three of you," I said. "I never asked you for anything. You're just looking to blackmail me."

I felt like I was defending myself, but no one was really attacking. Attack me? These three harmless beings?

"We're part of two different worlds," I said. "Two worlds that coexist, but can't overlap. When they do overlap, there's nothing but unhappiness and ruin. In both worlds."

"Richard has nothing to lose," she said.

Was this a threat, or was Anne simply stating a fact? I stopped to consider just what the relationship was between the three of them - Anne, Richard, and Sally. She repeated herself.

"When are you coming back?"

She pulled her skirt up over her thighs in order to attach one of her nylons. She revealed more than was necessary and as I watched the shadows move across her skin I knew that I had better hit the road. My anger was now turning into something else. I quietly moved past the table, keeping an eye on Richard's steady breathing.

"Give me the money," said Anne, keeping her voice low. "Richard needs to eat."

"And you?" I asked. "Don't you eat?"

She shook her head.

"I don't need any money. I've got people who help me make ends meet."

I stood there, uneasy. Why should I feel uneasy? I dug into my pocket and pulled out a bill. I looked at it. A ten-dollar bill.

"Here," I said.

"Thanks, Dan. Richard'll be happy."

"Don't call me Dan."

"Why not?" she asked, softly.

Why not? Of course she couldn't understand that Sheila says "Dan" in exactly the same way, with a little drawl. Too bad. She should have known.

I left the room without further ado. Anne made no effort to stop me.

I passed through the humid hallway, agitated by a variety of feelings which all congealed into an almost palpable uneasiness. I was suddenly struck by such a forceful sensation, a need to change, to leave my apartment and search out another, to hide. I started to sweat. I was in the clutches of some sort of anguish: The anguish of a hunted man, or rather the anguish of the prey that is leaving traces for its hunter. Have you ever seen a rat at the moment when the cat removes its paw from the animal's tiny little back? It stays there, motionless, not even trying to flee. And the next blow from the cat's claw is as gentle as a kiss, a kiss of love, and there is love in the victim for its torturer because of the way in which the killer strikes the final blow.

Richard, beyond any doubt, truly loved me. When would the final blow come?

Still, ordinary mice can't defend themselves. Me, I've got my fists. And I know how to use a revolver. You never know when those things will come in handy.

VII

That evening I had no desire to linger around at Nick's. I was exhausted, morally even more so than physically, and watching these same imbeciles gambling and boozing the same way, night in and night out, was becoming continually harder to stomach.

Unsettling ideas, as vague as shadows, stirred within my soul. But whatever these phantoms were, they decided to take pity on me, for night came to a close quickly and without a hitch. I found myself alone in the street, which was all aglow in yellow light, and each time I passed the shadow of a new streetlamp it was like the second hand of a clock slowly ticking away. In the darkness, the city was swarming with its unrelenting buzz and I picked up my step. I was pushed along by a curious impatience that seemed to be drawing me toward Sheila.

I didn't head straight into the bedroom. Instead, I entered silently and made my way to the bathroom where the window was open. I got undressed and took a shower, but this strange feeling that had come over me, like an intense state of drunkenness, left me impervious to the cool water, and I became aware of this as I wiped off my cold skin with the towel.

I threw my clothes down and passed by Sheila. She was sleeping, completely uncovered. Her pajama top gave way to her perfect breasts and her flowing locks partially covered her face. I stretched out alongside her and took her in my arms to kiss her, as I did every night. Without opening her eyes, she rose to a state of semi-consciousness and gave me a few kisses. She then offered herself up to my impatient hands. I completely undressed her. Her eyelids remained obstinately closed, but I knew they would open once she felt the crushing force of my weight. I caressed her cool arms and her nicely rounded hips. Stirred to by my caresses, she started murmuring soft little words.

I continued to kiss her and touch her warm, firm body. A few minutes passed. She was obviously waiting for me to take her, but I froze. I couldn't move. I couldn't do a thing. Sheila had not yet realized what was happening, and as for me, I had just become aware that her kisses left me cold, that the touch of her skin meant nothing to me, and that all that I was doing was being done mechanically, out of habit. I still loved her body, the firmness of her long legs, and the golden triangle that was her belly. And I truly loved the fleshy, brown points of her rounded breasts. But I loved her with a love that was now inert, in the same way one loves a photograph.

"What's wrong, Dan?" she said.

She spoke without opening her eyes. Her hand, which was resting on my shoulder, now started to make its way down the length of my arm.

"Nothing," I said. "I had a lot of work today."

"You have a lot every day," she said. "Don't you love me tonight?"

She pressed her body more forcefully into mine and I

THE DEAD ALL HAVE THE SAME SKIN

could feel her hand searching for it. I gently broke free.

"I'm just thinking about something," I said. "I have a lot on my mind. I'm sorry."

"Problems with Nick?"

There was not even a hint in her voice that she had the slightest interest in any problems I might have. She knew exactly what she wanted and felt frustrated because she wasn't getting it. And frankly I understood how she felt. I tried to think about something stimulating. I tried to imagine Sheila's body while we made love, her mouth half-open, her glittering teeth, and those throaty little moans that were like a soft cooing escaping through her lips as her head tossed from right to left and her nails dug into my back. She waited, not completely awake but conscious enough to know that something not quite right was happening to me.

"Yeah," I said. "I've got problems with Nick. He seems to think I'm getting too expensive to have around."

"He's the one who doesn't bring in enough clients," said Sheila.

"I can't tell him that."

"And you don't mind dealing with clients that don't bring in a lot of dough."

She moved away and I made no effort to pull closer to her. I felt bad. I was worried, and I continued to desperately search through my mind, on the lookout for some sort of memory. I replayed those evenings spent at Nick's and I saw all the girls that I'd taken to the telephone booths, all those blondes and brunettes whose touch seemed to give me strength.

These encounters really didn't wear me out. These brief little trysts with women whom I didn't love, women who saw in me the same thing I saw in them — a convenient partner ready for a little action — generally increased my desire for Sheila. It was as if this awareness of mine about the utter physicality of our desires made me hold on with even greater intensity to the woman I loved with all my soul.

And what a beautiful soul it was. The soul of a bouncer at a joint called *Nick's*.

My body was cold and flaccid, and my anxious muscles, agitated by cramps, jumped around like wild beasts beneath my skin.

"Sheila..." I murmured.

She didn't respond.

"Sheila, you're wrong to hold this against me."

"You're drunk. Leave me alone."

"I haven't been drinking, Sheila. I swear."

"I wish you had been. I wish it was that."

She spoke in low tones, tense, on the verge of tears. Sheila, I loved you so much.

"It's not that important," I said. "But I'd like very much for you to believe me. Maybe I'm wrong to get so worked up like this..."

"Even if Nick took all your money, Dan, that's still no reason to scorn me."

I made a desperate effort to get excited, to imagine some erotic scenes, to dissipate this unhealthy torpor which had glued my inert body to the sheets of our bed. I'd made love to Maxine and the others a good twenty times. And twenty times I'd come home with my spirits soothed, happy to find my wife and happy to satisfy her, because each time I tapped into a newfound force upon contact with her perfect body.

I couldn't. Nothing.

"Sheila," I said. "Forgive me. I don't know what you're thinking, what you could be imagining, but it's not because of another woman, or any women for that matter."

She was crying now, a light but rapid stream of tears.

"Oh, Dan... You don't love me anymore... Dan... You..."

I leaned over her. I kissed her. I did what I could. Some women can be calmed down this way and I truly wanted to make Sheila happy, but she pushed my head away violently and hid herself in the sheets, sheltering herself from my suffering.

I said nothing. It was dark in the room. I listened. The sound of her sobbing diminished and the steady softness of her breathing indicated to me that she had fallen asleep.

I carefully got out of bed and went back to the bathroom. My shirt was there, hanging on the wall. I grabbed it and took a big breath.

I was still saturated with the odor of Sally and Anne. I felt my body harden.

I dropped my shirt and moved my hands over my face. The odor had almost dissipated, yet it was still there somehow, vague and strong. Once again I saw Anne and Sally and our bodies, all entangled in that humid basement of the Harlem bistro.

Across the way, in the bedroom, Sheila slept. I hadn't asked myself if it was cheating to have indulged my desires with the girls at Nick's, banging professionals right in their clients' cars, even right under the noses of those same Johns. But now I understood that I was wrong and that I had committed an unpardonable act, because I was betraying her with my mind, and my body was now numb to her touch.

I tried to reassure myself. O.K. Maybe it's possible that sleeping with Blacks is more draining than with Whites, and that I simply needed a little rest. But the tenseness of my body bitterly revealed to me that this was not the case. In fact, the contrary was true, and the images that now passed through my mind were far from any peaceful blue waters of a comforting lake.

I got into the bathtub and pulled the chain — ice cold water this time to calm me down — because I didn't dare take advantage of this state I was in to wake up Sheila and chase away her suspicions.

I was afraid. I was afraid that this time she wouldn't stand up to the competition.

I got out of the bathtub feeling broken, my limbs defeated and overwhelmed, again morally more so than physically.

I got back into bed and lay in the shadows, wounded by something that I feared I understood all too well, and then sleep finally took me.

VIII

It was an unsettling sleep. I was tormented by nightmares, and despite my fatigue I was awake well before Sheila was because I felt, rather confusedly, that I had better get going before she started asking new questions that would steer last night's discussion into even worse territory. Our child was asleep in the adjoining room, so I had to move quickly because the noise from the streets always woke him up at around seven in the morning.

I shaved hastily, changed my clothes, and threw the soiled ones from last night into the hamper. I put on a light suit and left.

I had breakfast in a café. I took my time. Still, I had an entire day to kill before showing up for work at Nick's.

I stepped into a telephone booth and called Sheila.

"Hello?"

"Hello. It's Dan," I said. "How you doing?"

"Didn't you have any breakfast?"

"I had to get going," I explained. "It's that business that I told you about last night."

She didn't respond. I was overcome by a cold sweat at the thought that she might hang up.

"Oh, yeah..." she finally said. "I remember."

She pronounced each word in an icy tone.

"I won't be back. I'm headed straight to Nick's. I've got several people to see this morning."

"Be careful they're not wearing too much lipstick," she shot back.

Then she hung up. Fine. I set the receiver back down and left the booth.

A whole day to kill until five p.m. A long haul.

Take a walk. Maybe go to the movies.

Look for an apartment.

I smiled at the idea. Not a real jovial smile. It was another pathetic reminder, the cutting pain of a wound still fresh and so superficial that you're almost ashamed to even pay attention to it.

I tried not to think about these things that were gnawing at me with such force. It was a force so profound that I was able — as people often are in great catastrophes — to cut myself off, to become detached and remain almost indifferent.

In the beginning I was afraid of Richard. I risked losing everything: my job, my wife, my son, my entire life. I had lived day after day in fear. I tried everything. I even decided to confront my brother, face-to-face.

I finally met with him. To my misfortune, he wasn't alone. This confrontation with him had led to me discovering the essence of my being. Yes. I was now afraid of myself. The danger emanated from my own body, this body which was now rising against its master and driven by an instinct that I refused to recognize.

Say that Richard betrays me, that I lose my job, my wife, and my son. So be it. Yet if I held on to myself a chance still remained: a chance that I could win it all back.

On the other hand, if my own flesh betrayed me I would be left with utter nothingness.

I turned around and spotted a girl a bit too well dressed for this neighborhood at this hour. It was sunny out. I was alive.

I thought about Sheila.

I walked into a bar. The bartender was in shirtsleeves and wore a white apron. He was cleaning the counter with a grimy rag. Sawdust was strewn over the tile floor.

"Whiskey!" I said.

He served me without saying a word.

"Nice day, hey?" I added. "So what's the buzz this morning?"

"No buzz," he said. "Just the same old same old."

"Better play it safe with old Bob Whitney out there."

"He'll con 'em all," said the bartender.

The man didn't seem to be very talkative.

"What's there to do around here at eight in the morning?" I asked.

"Nothing," he responded. "That's to say nothing but work."

"I've got nothing to do until five this afternoon," I said, swallowing down my whiskey.

I was really having a hard time getting used to the booze.

Over in front of the counter there was a staircase that led to the second floor. You could hear the commotion of someone cleaning up with a mop and bucket. I looked over and saw a fat nigger woman in a black and white cotton blouse kneeling on the last step, her big ass swaying rhythmically back and forth.

"Another whiskey," I told the bartender.

What to do at eight in the morning? I caught sight of a juke box.

"What have you got in the juke box?"

"Dunno."

I gave up. I felt discouraged.

"What do I owe you?"

"A dollar."

I paid and left. I hit the closest subway station, bought a

paper, and waited for the train. It was crowded and I felt less alone. Still, all these people were going somewhere. They had lives. Me, I was living on the border, between races, both of which were ready to reject me. I was going nowhere. There was nothing in the paper. I left it on the train and stepped out.

I had gotten off near Harlem, almost as if by chance.

I walked into the first dry cleaning shop I found.

"Hello," I said.

"Hello, Sir."

There were two of them, some Jew and his helper. I took off my clothes in a little booth and waited while they got my pants ready. I would have to stay there. That would kill half an hour. What else could I do? Get my shoes shined? Five minutes. Have something to eat? That wouldn't kill enough time either.

A girl. A white girl. Just to give it a try.

I started to get impatient.

"Move it," I yelled at the dry cleaner. "I've got a hot date with Betty Hutton."

"I'll get you a little ice to cool you down," responded the man in the same tone of voice. "It'll be ready in a second. Don't mess 'em up. The crease on these pants is as sharp as a razor."

"I'll sit on my knees," I said.

"That'll crease 'em from behind," said the dry cleaning man.

I didn't press the issue. The guy was just the opposite of that bartender at the bistro. He was really laying it on. I waited. The only thought on my mind was a white girl.

I knew where to find them. One of the hostesses from Nick's lived nearby. I took her home at least once a week. She was a real moneymaker, that one. Nick was a lucky dog. Still, I decided to stop off for five minutes with the shoeshine man first.

IX

She opened the door herself, rubbing her eyes.

"Hey!" I said. "All alone?"

"Who do you take me for?"

"For my pal," I said. "Can I come in?"

"Of course."

"I'm not bothering you, am I?"

"O.K. if I get dressed in front of you?" she said.

"Take it easy," I said, "There's no need to hurry."

She looked at me and sort of squinted, then pulled back a lock of hair that was blocking her view.

"What do you want?" she said. "This is the first time you've come around here at this hour."

"I wanted to see you."

I put my coat on the table and sat down next to her.

"You're a nice little dish, you know," I said.

"You know what I'm like. This is nothing new."

"I just mean you're alright."

"You're a little funny this morning, Dan."

"Does it bother you?"

"Does what bother me?"

"That I came over..."

"I'd like to know why you came."

"Don't play the fool," I said.

She was within reach of my hands and I pulled her toward me. She didn't even try to close up her robe. She just let herself go. No resistance.

"You're a strange guy, Dan," she said.

"How's that?"

"Nobody at Nick's knows anything about you."

"Just what do they need to know?"

She took a while to answer and I passed the time by unsnapping her bra. She was maybe twenty-nine, but not any older. Nick always had nice, fresh meat.

"Where are you from?"

"Here and there..." I said, vaguely.

"Chicago?"

"Yeah, that's it."

"That's funny," she murmured. "Those Chicago guys always have to get tanked before they touch us. They're afraid to even try if they don't booze it up first."

"But you girls know how to work them," I said.

"We don't hustle the ones we find pleasing," she said provocatively, moving closer to me.

I was still sitting on the table, just at the right height for me to kiss her breasts. That lasted a good five minutes. She closed her eyes and pressed her perfumed flesh against my lips. With a simple movement, I moved to undress her. But she was already ahead of me. I'd taken off the transparent bra that was beneath her robe and her belly was completely hairless, naked, and tanned.

"You're funny..." she said once more, breaking away. "You're not going to stay sitting on that table, are you?"

"Where are you from?" It was now my turn.

"Brooklyn."

She laughed and grabbed me by the wrists in order to get me on my feet.

"I'm certainly not going to tell you I was born in the ritziest house on Central Park South."

"I don't need you to tell me that. Just tell me that you've got a nice body."

She stretched her limbs.

"Not bad."

I took off my jacket and she went over to lie on the bed. I removed my shoes and the rest of my clothes. She had lit a cigarette and was casually smoking, watching me out of the corner of her eye. I was ready to join her but she stopped me.

"You'll find some whiskey in the kitchen."

"I don't drink," I answered. "Not often."

I still had the taste of alcohol in my mouth from an hour ago.

"You look like you need it," she jeered.

I knew quite well that she was giving me the once over.

"Don't be afraid," I told her. "It works when it has to."

"I thought that you might be needing a little fuel," she said.

"The tank's full."

"Well, let's get going."

She reached over the side of the bed and crushed out her cigarette in an ashtray that was lying on the carpet. I moved closer and stretched out alongside her. I caressed her for a while. She said nothing. She didn't even look at me.

I started to wonder what was happening to me. I tried to kiss her, all over her body. Usually, that got me going, even when I was tired.

Nothing.

I kept at it, knowing that she was starting to get a little annoyed with my kisses. Her naked belly was warm and firm, like a gilded prune lying in the sun.

I suddenly pulled back. She smelled distinctly and decidedly like detergent.

To hell with it. I'd just as soon sleep with a washing machine.

I got back up. She had her two hands wrapped around her head and was turned to one side. A little smile unveiled her white teeth, and her fingers, with nails painted the color of steers' blood, tightened up into little balls in her beckoning palms. Her chest heaved forth with an intense rhythm.

She now understood that I was leaving and jumped out of bed.

"Dan! What's wrong?"

"Nothing."

"Stay with me."

"No."

"Why? Please, Dan..."

"You were right," I said. "I can't. It's not your fault. I wanted to be sure, and now, unfortunately, I am."

"Dan, please... You've got me all worked up!"

"Oh, alright," I said. "Get back in bed. I'll take care of it."

She spread herself out on the mattress and I sat down next to her. I did my best. It wasn't too much fun, but there certainly are some duties a lot less pleasurable. In any case, she was clean. In a couple of minutes I saw her body contract and offer itself up. Her fists tightened and then opened again, and she lay on her back, calm and relaxed.

"Dan…" she murmured. "My sweet little Dan."

"O.K.?"

"I really like that. A lot."

"Well, I'm glad you enjoyed it," I said.

"It wasn't too disgusting, Dan?"

"Oh," I mumbled, "It was either that or go to the track."

"You're a nasty brute, Dan. But would you like to, you know, do it again?"

"I don't see the need," I said. "The effect, as far as I'm concerned, is rather disappointing."

"Not for me." she said. "As for you, I don't care."

"Same thing I was thinking," I said. "I came to your place to find out if I could still do it. I've got the answer. I can't."

"You're enough for me."

"Thanks. Have you ever tried sleeping with a chick? I've got the feeling it'd be right up your alley."

"Well, I'd like to try," she said. "Do you think it would be similar?"

"It would for me, certainly."

"Don't go crazy on me, Dan. You know, there are pharmaceutical products."

"That's all bullshit," I said. "I mean, at my age? You know what I mean."

I could sense that we were speaking in a manner that was much more amicable than usual. Funny. Maybe women like impotents. A man, a real man, that makes them afraid. They're afraid of getting hurt. An impotent man, well, that's more like a close girlfriend.

"It happens to everyone," she said. "It's my business to know."

"You should remember that nine out of ten times your clients are shitfaced," I said. "Nothing like getting plastered if you want to shut down your motor."

"Well, that happens too," she admitted. "But you don't drink. Maybe you've just become bored with it all. Have you ever thought about doing it with a man?"

She smiled when she saw the scowl on my face.

"Fuck you," I said. "I'd rather screw a horse."

"You wouldn't be half-bad at it," she gibed.

That also was the kind of remark a good friend would make. I didn't respond.

"You might try something else," she said. "Two, three women..."

"Or a boarding school, perhaps? With you along?" I said.

"Or a black chick. I hear they're..."

"Shut your face!..."

Now I was infuriated. Truly. Crazy infuriated.

She looked at me. She didn't understand. Lucky for her she kept her mouth shut. Otherwise I would have given her a good smack.

I turned away and got dressed in silence. I heard her move around softly on the bed. My wrath was diminishing.

"Dan," she said, softly. "I'm sorry..."

She really was a decent girl, deep down.

"It's O.K.," I said. "It's nothing."

"Don't beat yourself up over this, Dan. I really... I mean... well, thanks."

Good God! That whore had almost gotten me turned on. Just what makes them tick?

Where do they come up with this stuff?

She stood up, and with light little steps made her way over to the armchair to fetch her robe.

"Want some coffee, Dan?"

I buttoned my pants.

"Yes, please."

I grabbed her just as she passed by me. She was seized by a sudden jolt of fear and she stared at me with a worried look in her eyes. I wrapped my arms around her shoulders and kissed her very gently.

"Thanks, little sister."

Sufficiently reassured, she returned my kiss and went off to her miniscule kitchen where I could hear her light the gas and look for some dishes. She was singing a popular little number.

I left my jacket where it was and dove into the armchair. I was spent. Wiped out. You'd have needed a wheelbarrow to push me around.

X

She came back a little while later with a tray containing a complete lunch. While she was busy setting up the plates and glasses on the tiny folding table, I asked her:

"Now really? What I did pleased you just as much as the other times?"

"What other times?" she declared. "You haven't visited me all that often here."

"Anyway, you didn't seem to really get off," I said.

"Good God!" she responded, "There's a lot that's gone on here since then, you know. But I'm telling you, what you did for me a little while ago..."

She blushed.

"I don't like talking about it, Dan. I might be a hooker and all, but I don't want to talk about it. When I do it for money it's not the same."

"Don't you have some man who could take care of you, I mean in the way you want to be taken care of?" I said.

"No." she said. "I had a man once, and he was the one who got me into this racket, Dan. He was a filthy bastard. He just wanted my dough. I thought he loved me, so of course I was happy to do it for him. But he was just laughing at me the whole time. I never saw him again. He had other chicks in his stable, but he had to leave New York after his run-in with the Luciano brothers."

"So why have you kept it up?" I asked her.

"You can't just sit around and wait to die of hunger, Dan. And the work isn't so bad. Why do you continue doing what you do?"

"I've got a wife and a kid," I told her. "I love them. As you said, the work's not so bad."

"You're a lucky man," she said. "But me, I guess deep down inside I prefer to be by myself."

"Lots of girls live together," I said. "It seems that would be less dreary."

"I don't know, Dan. I'd like it better if..."

She hesitated.

"Why'd you stop?" I said, pouring myself a cup of coffee.

"I'd like to have a guy like you, Dan. Strong, yet tender. And if it were so, you could do to me what you did a while ago."

She sat on my lap, unconcerned with the cup of coffee I was holding and which was quivering dangerously on my thighs.

"But you don't want that, Dan."

Now that was something else. I come over, I tell this girl that I want to sleep with her, I can't get it going, but even so, despite that, she sticks to me like flypaper. Women are insane.

"I've got a wife and a kid, I'm telling you."

A sense of shame shot through me as I thought of Sheila. Sheila, whom I'd so cruelly let down the night before. Sheila. In an instant, I saw myself: me with this hooker and Sheila with another man. My heart bled with rage. It was always like that. You're married and you sleep with other girls. Absolutely no scruples. But to imagine your wife with another man — you could annihilate the entire world. There's nothing anyone can do. It's all beside the point, anyway. A man never cheats on his wife.

"You're sweet," I told her. "But I don't want that. And you deserve better than some impotent guy."

I passed the time caressing one of her breasts and the little pink point held up the transparent silk of her negligee. She made a clumsy gesture and half of my coffee ended up spilling over into the saucer.

"Stop," I said. "Be careful. Get up. Hurry and get dressed. I'll take you to the movies."

"Super!" she said. "It's as if we were fiancés."

"Exactly," I agreed.

I was surely not going to explain to her why we were going to the movies. Neither to her nor to anyone else. I didn't even want to think about it myself.

XI

It was two in the afternoon when she finished dressing. It always takes longer than you think. Still, it suited me just fine. There would be more people at the cinema.

Anyway, I had chosen the theatre that I wanted to take her to. It was a small place, located next to a high school for girls, and always packed. Obviously, there was a chance that my project would fail miserably, but I still had a back-up plan in store.

We left her apartment and took the elevator to the first floor. I gave her the once-over, rather stealthily. Despite her youth, there was something in the way she carried herself, her manner of dress, that made it impossible to tell just exactly what she was. An idea came to me: the idea that I had succeeded in concealing something all the more shameful about myself. I had succeeded and I would continue to succeed.

"But to what end was I succeeding?" I asked myself, sarcastically. All this effort. And for what? For those years I spent working at Nick's? And now I turn out to be impotent. Shit!... Well, I was calm for the moment. It would come back to me soon enough.

Funny. Last night with Sheila I was shattered. And a while ago, with this girl — even though she was a bit sharp with me — I had lost my cool. But now, I felt as tranquil as ever.

I knew what I was going to do.

She was walking at my side. Pretty little thing. The legs, the breasts, the face. She had it all.

You really have to know how to choose your alibis.

We arrived at the theatre and got a couple of tickets.

The usher's flashlight cut a hole into the shadows and I followed him down the nickel-plated staircase and over the plush carpet. He looked at my tickets.

"The only seats left are separated," he said. "You can switch places later."

Lady Luck was really smiling on old Dan.

She took her seat and I sat down two rows back.

Ten minutes later I got up and headed quietly towards

the rear. I hit the exit and was now on the street. An empty
taxi passed by. I started to stretch out my hand.

No. No taxi. The subway.

I looked at my watch. Plenty of time.

I dashed towards the subway.

XII

I cast a nonchalant glance from right to left and then
entered the dirty little bistro where I'd met Richard the
night before. Blacks, mulattos, even Whites. A real no man's
land.

Upon entering, I deliberately tipped my hat over my eyes
and headed straight for the staircase.

The man behind the counter barely even raised his eyes
as I passed. I was seized by the acrid humidity in the hallway and took deep breaths to get accustomed to it.

I saw the door, and making as little noise as possible,
walked in without knocking. Richard was sleeping,
sprawled out across the filthy sofa. There was an empty bottle on the table. Anne and Sally were nowhere in sight. My
luck was almost too good to be true. Still, the odor of the
women impregnated the room. In spite of myself, I could
feel my body react, and I mean react in the way I couldn't
get it to react with Sheila or that whore from Nick's place.

Richard. He was going to pay for this.

I jumped on top of him and throttled his neck.

He didn't even have the time to cry out. I squeezed with
all my force, and I could feel his hyoid bone start to bend.

Utter perfection. Not even a mark. I let him loose, and
leaving him no time to catch his breath, covered his face
with one of the torn-up cushions from the sofa.

And then I pushed. His gnarled body twisted around

every which-way as he tried to escape. I spread my body out, almost directly over him, trying to control him, crushing his legs between mine. I clutched at him desperately, but somehow he was able to give me a painful kick to the groin. My head was spinning and I felt like vomiting, but I kept hold of the cushion and succeeded in pinning Richard to the discolored fabric. He tightened his hands around my right wrist and tried to push back the cushion, but I had shifted my arm under the back of his neck. He wasn't about to escape from this vice-grip.

He struggled for a good five minutes. I started to lose my strength, and my eyes seemed to be dancing around in their sockets. I could feel the sweat pouring out of me, trickling down my skin, sticking to my shirt and covering my contracted muscles.

Richard's hand remained wrapped around my wrist, but his fingers were no longer squeezing into my flesh. With a burst of force, I broke free.

No more need to struggle. It was over.

I left the cushion covering his face and quickly rifled through his pockets. A dirty little notebook. Some coins. A few things too disgusting to name. Some subway tickets. The notebook was it. Nothing else represented any threat.

I lifted the cushion. Not a pretty sight. I went over to the table and carefully picked up the bottle with my handkerchief. After spilling the rest of the alcohol over his face and clothes, I placed the bottle beside him.

Not much chance they'd figure this one out. Anyway, who the hell is going to worry whether some mulatto found in the basement of a rotten little dive in Harlem really died from heart failure?

Not the cops, in any case.

I looked around the room. Everything was in order. I fixed up Richard's clothes. I'd been careful not to mess them up too much when I was digging through his pockets. I'd done a real nice job. He was hard and cold now, like a block of cement. That's how it is when you die in a real struggle.

I made my way out quickly. I had the feeling that a door had opened behind me. I turned around. Nothing. I shrugged my shoulders and went up the staircase. I walked across the room and went outside.

Time. One hour had flown past. Good. I headed back towards the subway.

I was back at the theatre in no time. There was nobody watching the emergency exit. I pushed against the door marked "No Entrance." Another humid hallway. It made me think about the one I'd just been in.

I had no remorse.

I peeped through the little window of the door that led to the seats. There was no one in front.

I pushed the door open. I found myself suddenly startled and enveloped by the actors' voices. The usher flashed his light at me. He quickly walked over.

Stupid move. Too bad. But I had an excuse.

"What are you doing?"

I handed him my ticket.

"The restrooms?"

"Not that way, Sir," he said, looking at my rumpled ticket. "Over there."

"Thanks," I said.

Two minutes later I went back to my seat. It was taken, but the one right in front was open. I sat down and tapped my date's shoulder.

"Hello!" I said.

She grabbed my hand, as if I were a phantom, and let out a muffled cry.

"Dan!" she murmured. "You scared me!"

She let go almost immediately and was once again lost in

the imaginary world of the screen.

It was just getting better and better.

Still, it gave me the creeps when she squeezed my wrist in the exact same place Richard had done so an hour earlier.

To hell with it.

Better not to think about those kinds of things.

XIII

Everything had gone down exactly as planned.

In the papers the next morning there was a little paragraph, a few lines, and then nothing more.

Once again, I found myself lying next to Sheila. She had just fallen asleep. As for me, my state hadn't improved at all.

There was nothing to do at Nick's that afternoon either. I hadn't even made an effort.

I tried to get a hold of myself, to explain it all. But that task appeared to be beyond my ability.

Why couldn't I make it with these women? With my wife? Last night's words resonated in my ears:

"Or a black chick. It seems that they're…"

Maybe it was the contact with these two Black girls that made me sense, in the very depths of my being, that I was Black. It was a feeling that carried with it all of the ancestral terror – the fear of a nigger when faced with white women.

It's what they call a complex. Maybe that's it. But I didn't have any damn complex until a night ago, or any feeling of being Black. I felt as white as ever.

So maybe there isn't any such thing as an instinctive complex? Or perhaps there is?

Still, I kept on deliberately searching in the wrong places because, in all reality, I knew what I wanted and I ended up admitting it to myself. I tried it with Sheila and no luck.

Then another White girl. Nothing.

Now it was time to find a Black woman. Alright. Time to take the plunge. I had to know.

I crawled out of bed furtively, as I had done a night ago, without a sound.

It was maybe three in the morning. I'd find plenty of nightclubs open.

And I'd find mulattos.

I wanted one who was real dark. Sweaty and fat.

I quickly got dressed and closed the door as I left. I was counting on getting back before Sheila awoke.

I walked about three blocks before I found a taxi. I slipped him an address, some place near Harlem. It wasn't really easy for a white guy to get what I was looking for in that part of town. But I hadn't been a bouncer these last five years for nothing, and I knew where to go.

It's not all that rare, really - whites who want to change the shade of their skin.

XIV

The joint didn't look too inviting. It was a crummy little dive, like a lot of others. I entered. Not many people inside. Three or four women, five or six men, and the bartender, wearing a disgusting jacket.

I ordered a highball. The bartender served it up. As he leaned over to hand me my change, I murmured:

"Any chicks looking for a date?"

He looked at me suspiciously.

"Ike the Lion sent me," I said.

"O.K." he said, reassured.

His black mug had lightened up a bit now. He bent over, rifled through some bottles, and stood back up. He handed me a crumpled up little card.

"Two blocks from here," he indicated. "Say that Jack sent you."

"Thanks," I shot back.

I dropped him a hefty tip and left. Two blocks. Five minutes. I walked in. It was a rather nice looking building. The hallway was dimly lit and the concierge was asleep at the front desk. I walked up six flights. I followed the instructions that the bartender had penciled onto the card and rang twice. The woman who opened the door was about thirty years old, well dressed and wearing too much jewelry. It would have taken a pretty sly customer to figure out if she were a mulatto or simply Mexican. And I was just sly enough for that.

"Come in," she said. I passed her the card and told her that Jack had sent me.

She shut the door and I followed her. She closed the curtain behind us and we went through another door and drew back a different curtain. I was now in a rather nicely furnished room.

I sat down in a leather armchair.

"You want a really dark woman?" she asked.

"Pretty dark," I said.

Her look was making me a little uncomfortable.

"Not too thin?" she added.

She was sporting a little grin.

"I can choose, can't I?" I asked.

"Sure," she replied. "I'll send a couple in for you."

I waited as she disappeared behind another door. My heart was beating more rapidly than usual.

She returned almost immediately, pushing in front of her a strong, dark-skinned black girl and a young mulatto a lot lighter, thin and tall, with perfectly normal features. The first was maybe twenty-five. The second couldn't have been a day over sixteen.

"Here's Rosie," said the madam. "And this one's Jo," she added, placing her right hand on the shoulder of the younger girl.

Rosie's dress really gave way to her cleavage and her skin was all aglow in the dimly lit room. She was smiling with her thick, heavily painted lips. The other one just stood observing me, immobile.

The madam took note of my hesitation.

"You can take them both," she told me.

I pulled out my wallet. She came over and I paid her.

"Rosie, show this gentleman the way."

I followed them into a third room, completely empty except for a huge bed and a sink tucked away into a sort of alcove with a curtain around it.

A dark carpet covered the floor.

The room was quite somber, lit up simply with a tiny pink lamp.

Rosie was already undressed and stretched out across the bed. I was suddenly suspicious and glanced over at Jo. Finally convinced, I started to laugh.

"You can leave," I said. "I don't go for boys."

He smiled, not at all embarrassed. Rosie started to laugh as well.

"Your boss put one over on me," I added.

"Let him stay," said Rosie.

I took off my coat. Jo opened up his dress and let it fall to his ankles. He stood there, completely nude and indecent.

"Let him stay," repeated Rosie with a chuckle, "you won't regret it."

"I'm not into that kind of stuff," I said.

"Ever tried?" asked Jo, coldly.

I was flabbergasted.

"There's no way I'll try that," I said.

"Come on," said Rosie. "Don't worry yourself. You know, I can make love in the French style…"

"Me too," I said.

I took off the rest of my clothes. I no longer had any reason to doubt my abilities. Still, I really didn't want that boy in the room. But then again… maybe there was another solution.

I saw now that I was wrong to have gotten so worried. Deep down, I truly suspected it: That I needed a Black woman to make a man of myself once more. But now I really wanted to be honest with myself.

No use sleeping with Rosie. I knew what the result would be. No doubt about it if I restricted myself to looking only at Rosie.

But if I restricted myself to simply observing the two of them, then I would be able to defend myself before Sheila. And Sheila was indispensable to me. It wasn't worth the trouble to play any games here.

Rosie was waiting for me. I sat down on the side of the bed.

"Come on over, Joe," I said. "I'll watch you."

"You come too," said Rosie, excited.

"I'll watch," I repeated.

Without a trace of uneasiness, the young boy moved towards the girl, who made an offering of her arched loins. Gently but firmly, he took her before my very eyes. They seemed to be acting out an inexorable rite. Rosie's legs stiffened and tensed, and I was rather fascinated by the whole thing. I smelled the scent of the woman and watched the young man's muscles at play. After a moment or so, Rosie pushed him away. She looked at me.

"Come on," she said. "At the same time."

"No," I said.

With no phony concern for propriety, she caressed Jo.

"Why?" she asked. "I'm not sick. Neither is Jo."

"It's not that," I said. "I just needed to verify something. I'm satisfied."

She jumped off the bed and onto her knees, where she tried to grab hold of me. I felt the lightening-hot contact as her mouth greedily enveloped mine, but I yanked her back by her frizzy shock of hair and broke loose. I rose. It was hard to resist. It was as if I was bedazzled. I wanted her so badly that every part of my body ached. And it was obvious that Rosie needed me as much as I needed her.

She threw herself violently against Jo, and all I could hear was their hurried panting and the gentle sound of their interlacing bodies.

I walked over to the alcove and found the sink. I leaned over and stuck my head under the faucet. I stayed there, under a stream of water, for several minutes, desperate and gasping for breath.

Neither Jo nor Rosie was paying any attention to me. I opened the door and left.

Once in the street, I started to catch my breath. I looked at my watch. It was five in the morning.

I made my way back home.

XV

Sheila's body was lying there like before, asleep in the same position. It was obvious that she hadn't moved a muscle since my departure.

I crept in beside her and enveloped her body before she had time to wake herself. She didn't open her eyes but instead clasped her hands behind my neck and gave way to my caresses, anticipating my desire.

Then she suddenly broke away, silent and weary, with a soft smile on her lips. I remained next to her, feeling uneasy because I knew I couldn't get it going again.

"Dan…" she murmured sleepily.

"Yes," I replied. "I'm sorry about last night. And tonight."

"Are you really that preoccupied, Dan?"

"I swear to you," I said. "But I think I've found a solution."

"It's funny…," she said. "Funny that these worries of yours have this effect on you."

Indeed it was funny. I would have never believed it.

"I was just a bit overworked," I said. "But that's all passed."

My thoughts drifted back to Rosie and Jo, back on that huge bed, and I started to get a bit stimulated. But Sheila was now almost completely asleep.

"No, Dan… Please, I'm dead tired."

"Why?" I asked, astonished. "Not over last night? That was nothing."

She hid her face in her hands.

"Dan… You have to forgive me."

"What?" I said.

"I'm tired, Dan… I… I don't know how to put it."

"You've found another man." I replied, curtly.

Her eyes were now wide open.

"Dan! You don't believe that. It's not that… I… I just can't bring myself to tell you, Dan."

"Well I'm not worried about it, whatever it is. Provided it's not some other guy."

"There's nobody else, Dan. It was… Well, it was me Dan, all alone."

I started to laugh. I was a little pissed off.

"Well, if that's all it is…" I said.

"Are you mad, Dan?"

"Not at all," I assured her. "After all, it was all my fault."

"You're angry. Don't hold this against me…"

She rested her head against my arm.

"Please Dan. Don't leave me feeling like this. I need you, Dan. I need *it*."

"You don't need it that much," I said, in a somewhat nasty little tone.

"Yes I do. It's not easy being alone. No fun at all. It's a real bore and a pain, quite frankly. Dan, if you left me for a whole week, I think I'd have to take drugs just to calm myself down. That, or I'd have to sleep with some other guy."

"That's just charming," I said.

I started to laugh. What a great outcome. Really. I had killed Richard because of that night. And if I should take ill, or be forced to leave New York, well then Sheila would abandon me. And what if they discover something? No. Surely they won't find anything… But what about the guy who took me to Richard's place that first time? Anne and Sally? The manager of that little bistro?

The criminal mentality is truly strange, I suddenly thought. People think they would be haunted by remorse, tormented by atrocious visions.

Fat chance. It's only with the greatest difficulty that you can force yourself to think about the consequences of your actions.

In reality, all that I'd done had left me feeling completely cold now. The only thing that mattered was what Sheila had just said to me.

Well I suppose I could take off for a couple of days, and then… But just what is it that's making me want to stay with her? Why can't I leave her without having that feeling of emptiness, the need to come back to her? I need to know that she's mine - that she's mine even if I'm not around and that I could see her if I wanted to…

Is that what love is?

If so, it's not much fun.

All in all, there's really nothing to do.

To have it come to this: a woman for whom, physically

speaking, I can no longer even get aroused. It had just been proven to me in such a brutal manner that I could no longer ignore it. I've got a woman who can't do without a man, to the point where she would replace me if I were imprudent enough to leave her alone for a couple of days.

And now I understood what it was all about. That's what makes you suffer.

I just had to imagine Sheila with another man. Or all alone. Oh, well. Too bad.

There's always the black girls. And no more Richard to worry about.

The Good Lord, Richard, has permitted me to be rid of you. I'll keep Sheila and you can go to hell.

Goodnight, Dan.

XVI

I left Nick's for a moment to run an errand. The paper boys were pushing a special edition.

I read, without really grasping their importance, the headlines on the first page: "Negro Crosses the Line to Kill his brother – The Victim's Mistress Makes the Accusation – Police are on the Lookout for Dan."

XVII

Anne quickly closed the door of the telephone booth and found herself back out on the street. Her knees went weak and she had to hide her trembling hands in order not to draw attention to herself.

She quickly made her way down the street and turned left at the corner. After about a block she saw the café where Sheila had agreed to meet her.

She walked in and sat down. It was the kind of place someone like her could go without causing too much of a scene.

She could hear the paperboys shouting about the special edition. The journalists hadn't wasted a second. Neither had the police.

The door opened and in strolled an attractive blonde. She was wearing the blue felt hat that she had mentioned on the telephone. She quickly glanced around and moved over in the direction of Anne.

"So you're Mrs. Parker?" asked Anne.

"Yes."

"I have some things to tell you. Is it alright if we stay here?"

"Why not?" Sheila replied, curtly.

"It's not easy to talk about this."

Sheila looked back at her and then reached for her purse. The young mulatto's face grew somber.

"I don't want any money. This is just about Richard."

"Oh, right… That nonsense. Dan's so-called brother."

"Well it's not just some stupid story," said Anne. "Let's get back to your place before it's too late. And don't make yourself too conspicuous. Dan will kill you, too."

"You're talking rubbish," murmured Sheila.

"I saw Dan kill his brother," said Anne. "Dan has black blood. He's black, you understand? He was afraid that Richard would tell you. He really cares about you, and he killed Richard because he was afraid. But I saw him when he left. Richard was my man."

She spoke in choppy, broken phrases, full of dread. Sheila's eyes grew wide with horror and disbelief.

"This is ridiculous," she said. "It must have been someone else. Dan is not black."

"He is," said Anne. "He's a quarter black. At least."

"*Ridiculous...*" *she repeated.* "*You'd be able to see it.*"
"*You know very well that those things aren't always visible,*" *said Anne.*
"*But Dan couldn't kill anybody! Much less his own brother.*"
"*Beating people up is his job!*" *she shot back sharply.* "*It would have been no problem for him. But I'll have my revenge.*"
She stood up, quickly approaching a state of panic that bordered on frenzy.
"*You're talking trash,*" *said Sheila.* "*None of this makes any sense.*"
"*Buy a paper,*" *said Anne.* "*It's all there. The police have already verified it.*"
"*Have they arrested him?*" *asked Sheila, suddenly pale as a ghost.*
"*They must be close.*"
"*Well why wouldn't they have brought him in before all this hit the papers?*"
"*Dan's boss must have paid off the cops,*" *said Anne.* "*They don't like scandals. They're probably waiting for him to leave.*"

XVIII

Dan hurriedly slipped a nickel to the paperboy and snatched up a copy. There was a picture of Anne, followed by the story. Luckily, there wasn't any photo of him.
He glanced to the right, then to the left. Just a crowd of innocuous passersby. A taxi was slowly approaching. As it made its way towards him he hailed it over and quickly slipped inside. In the rearview mirror he saw two men step off the curb and move in his direction. He told the driver to step on it.
"*Faster.*"
"*Where to?*" *asked the driver.*

"Turn here."

The driver followed his orders and the motor roared.

"Take a left at the next street," said Dan.

He fumbled through his pockets and pulled out a couple of dollars.

"Keep going. Slow down when you turn the corner."

"Straight ahead. Hurry."

The taxi stopped and he jumped out onto the sidewalk. Just opposite him was a subway station. He darted across the street and slipped inside.

A police car rounded the corner and hit its brakes.

Dan shrugged his shoulders. He calmly walked back out and headed in the opposite direction.

The trick was to not make it too evident that he was trying to hide.

It would be a mistake to get too far away from Sheila right now.

He thought to himself as he walked.

The girl. The one he was with the night before. She had made him some coffee. She had accepted his visit without asking a single question. Surely she wouldn't turn him in.

Usually she came into Nick's place at about ten at night.

He changed directions. Better to head straight there. He might be able to catch her.

He marched quickly through a sea of indifferent faces, lost in the crowd, trying to focus on the problem at hand.

He had to evade the cops.

But surely the best way to evade capture would be to not worry about them, almost as if they didn't exist.

XIX

In the entrance to her building, Muriel removed her gloves.

The sudden sound of the doorbell gave her a start. She turned on her heels and came back to the door. She unhooked the security chain and turned the doorknob.

In a furtive and rapid maneuver, Dan slipped inside the entryway and pushed back the lacquered panel of the door.

"Hi," he said. "You sure took your time getting back."

"You were waiting for me?" she asked, astonished.

"I was downstairs," he murmured. "Five and a half hours."

"Listen, do you think I sit around all day with nothing to do?" *She looked angry.*

"I need to stay here," he said bluntly.

"But Dan! You must be crazy... I have people over here all the time. I can't let you stay here."

"You would have let me stay last night."

"So you could have taken advantage of me..." *she shot back, brutally.*

"It's not like you didn't want it," he said, as he moved closer and seized her by the arm.

She grew pale.

"Don't squeeze me like that, you animal! Don't you understand..."

She fought back, twisting her arm, and broke free. She started to cry.

"Christ, Dan!... You're not aware of you own strength..."

He let go of her and lowered his head.

"Listen, Muriel. The cops are looking for me."

"What have you done?"

"Killed a guy. My brother. Read the papers."

Her jaw dropped.

"So it was you?"

He silently nodded.

"Listen Muriel," he continued, "That... well, it's not important. What I need now is to stay here. I can't leave the neighborhood."

"Why?"

"My wife. I need to stay in the neighborhood."

He shrugged his shoulders.

"Don't you see? I can't have a bunch of cops all over me like a cheap suit. Listen, Dan, you're a nice guy, but you've got to beat it, and tell me if you want me to…"

She stopped for a moment and then continued.

"Just get out. And hurry. I don't want any cops here. I know what jail is all about."

He looked at her but didn't seem to understand.

"Muriel, I really need to stay here. My wife is going to take off."

"Just leave your wife the hell alone. Have you even told her that you're black?

His face hardened and his breathing became labored.

"Don't say that again," he told her. "I'm telling you…"

Muriel moved away. Dan stood his ground, tense and motionless.

She bolted up, headed for the door to her room and slammed it shut. He flung himself forward, but the key had already made its way into the deadbolt.

The door began to crack. From the other side he could hear her start to move the furniture. There was a resounding shock against the door and then an explosive thud. A small crack appeared in the panel of the door and a fragment of wood broke loose.

Dan stopped. He looked at the wound he had inflicted on the wood. Muriel's voice rang out from the other side.

"Go! Go, or I'll call the police."

He could hear her pick up the phone.

Slowly, without turning around, he moved back. His hands slid over the doorknob. He was now back on the landing. His lips were moving, but his confused words were incomprehensible.

"Sheila…" he finally blurted out.

He almost called for the elevator, but then changed his mind

and walked down the stairs. He continued speaking to himself.
"I have to see her. I have to know."

He kept climbing down the stairs. His gait grew more assured as he approached the street. A quick glance revealed not a soul waiting outside and he left without drawing the least attention to himself.

After a few steps he fumbled through his pockets. He counted the money that he had left, roughly thirty-two dollars. Might as well be nothing.

He turned around and deliberately came back to the building he had just exited. The banister of the stairway gave way under the traction of his clenched fingers. The door was still open. Muriel hadn't dared to move.

He entered without the slightest sound, and then he violently slammed the door. He proceeded towards the second door, trying to calm his labored breathing.

He waited.

XX

Sheila moved through the streets like a somnambulist. She saw a paperboy and noticed, while digging through her handbag for a nickel, that she hadn't closed her purse.

She looked down at the newspaper, overcome by a sense of fear. There was a photo of the girl she had just encountered, and the story of the killer, with all those little details that newspapermen are able to uncover when they feel like taking the trouble to do so.

She decided not to return home. They would be waiting for her.

She turned around. There was a man reading his paper while walking and he suddenly stopped.

She came over to him.

"You're a policeman," she said.

He didn't bother to deny it. He smiled, reached into his pock-et, and showed her his badge.

"Lieutenant Cooper," he said. "I'm not really suspicious of you," he said, as if excusing himself.

He seemed strangely confused to have been spotted so quick-ly. He was a young man, and not at all disagreeable.

"You didn't look like you were going to try and make a break for it," he added. "That's the usual routine. We followed the Negro girl."

"Are the cops at my place?" asked Sheila. "Listen, please don't try and tell me they're not. Don't give me any of that business. Anyway, I don't want to go home. I don't want to run, and I'm…"

She hesitated.

"… I don't give a damn about what happens to Dan," she said decisively. "I'd like to call home. Can I?"

She smiled at him. She was a pretty girl, but a bit common. Big hips. Blonde, of course.

"Sure," said the man. "I'll keep you company."

This guy wouldn't be too hard to manipulate.

He accompanied her to the nearest phone booth and waited outside, far enough away so that he couldn't hear the conversa-tion. She smiled and turned her shoulders as she entered the booth and she left the door half open.

"Come in if you want," she said. "I have nothing to hide, you know. If someone's been screwed in this whole fiasco it's me!"

He stayed near the door, a bit embarrassed.

"I just need to tell the babysitter to take the kid to my mom's," she said. "Then I'll go with you to the police station. I suppose I should get an attorney. You guys should be able to recommend one. I have no intention of staying married to a criminal."

Cooper acquiesced.

"Let me make the call," he said. "The cops are at your place, so we can let the babysitter go. I'll tell them not to destroy anything

or remove your belongings," he added. "It'll be safer that way."

She moved out of the booth and gave him the number.

"Thank you," she said, forcing herself to speak with a tone of conviction.

She stared him straight in the eyes, which caused him to blush a little. She was tastefully dressed, unlike all the hookers he was used to rounding up. And her husband was a killer. Black. What a strange woman. Was this all her fault? He made the call and straightened everything out with a few words.

"Does..." he started to ask timidly.

"Does what?

"Does your husband have a criminal past? Do you know if he was involved in any criminal activity before he killed his brother?"

"No," said Sheila. "Why?

"Because maybe he could beat the rap if he found a good lawyer," said Cooper. "All we have is the deposition of that woman and the barman. There's enough to send him to the chair... but if the victim was trying to blackmail him... You see, there's something troubling in all this. Your husband seems to be, for all intents and purposes, White."

"So?" said Sheila.

"So it's a troubling case," said Cooper. "The truth is that you never know what a good lawyer can find. I don't know... maybe his mother cheated on his father, and maybe he's really white. People believe all too easily that Blacks can cross the line. They have to be reassured. What I mean is that here in New York, these things are different. Discrimination isn't so severe here, but in the south this will cause quite a row."

"I see," said Sheila.

"Maybe you know something else about him, something that we could use against him, to be sure to convict him, some other thing..."

"Do you realize what you're asking of me?" said Sheila.

"A while ago you said you didn't give a damn about what happened to him," Cooper reminded her.

"Of course," murmured Sheila. "But still, I lived with him for five years. We have a child."

She suddenly realized what was happening and looked at Cooper, stupefied.

"So tell me," she said. "They're going to arrest him, judge him and kill him?"

"I don't know," said Cooper, embarrassed.

"Christ!" said Sheila. "Christ Almighty!"

XXI

Muriel listened, uneasy. She hadn't called the police; she had confined herself to fidgeting with the telephone receiver. She had procured a revolver for herself and was now contemplating it with great anxiety. Even with the gun resting in her hands she felt little solace.

She heard someone pound violently on the door. Then, nothing. Dan must be on the lam. There's nothing left for him to do here. Funny to think that he would end up killing his brother while just the night before he was holding her in his arms. She made an effort to forget exactly what he had done with her during those moments. She could no longer decide if it had been pleasant or disgusting.

Dan must have left. But she would have liked to be sure of it.

She picked up the receiver and then hung it back up. She dialed the number of the police station, pretending to speak as if someone were on the other end. She gave the address and the details. She said "Thank you" and fidgeted with the phone once again.

The door cracked and broke open with single blow. The tables and chairs that were feebly piled up in front of the door came crashing down. Muriel didn't even have the time to take aim at Dan. She found herself crushed under his weight as he covered her lips with his cold, hard hands. She closed her eyes and gave up the struggle.

"Shut your mouth" he told her, emotionless and calculating. "Shut up or I'll strangle you. I'm going to take my hand away from your mouth, and if you make the smallest little gesture, I'll choke you to death. It won't take long. I guarantee it."

She could feel his grip loosen. Her lips and teeth hurt, and Dan's other hand must have left a bruise on her neck. Although she was no longer so afraid, he still perhaps wanted to kill her.

"Where's your money?" he murmured.

"I only have fifty bucks," she said.

"That's a bunch of crap," he said.

He spoke with the same neutral, emotionless voice.

"I swear, Dan…"

"Where's your purse?"

"It's not there. I only have ten or twelve dollars in my handbag."

She started to cry.

"Dan, I don't have much money. What do you want me to do?"

"Just give it to me. And hurry up."

She got up and made a move for the little revolver. Dan tightened his fist and let her have it in her right breast. She almost screamed, but Dan was back on his feet and his hand crushed her lips closed. He let go almost immediately. She could feel the blood in her mouth. Tears appeared in the corners of her makeup-stained eyes.

"Hurry," he repeated.

She remained motionless. Something was stopping her from obeying him – something that had emptied her muscles, left them flabby and inert, with no ability to react or defend herself.

In a cold gesture, Dan ripped away the top of her dress and started to take her clothes off. She tried to push back his hands.

"Did you know that a cigarette burn can leave quite a pretty little mark?" asked Dan.

"Dan! Please, I'm begging you!"

He let go of her.

"Give me the money. It's the last time I'll ask."

Now convinced, she walked over to the dresser and opened the first drawer. Dan was keeping a close eye on her. She fumbled through some silk garments and then handed Dan a roll of bills. He shoved them into his pocket without saying a word.

"You didn't call the cops," he said. "They'd have been here by now."

"No."

"I knew it," he said. "I was listening. You're not much of an actress."

She started crying again.

"Dan… I… I liked you a lot better last night. I don't feel well. You hurt me. I'm sure I'm injured somewhere."

"How much is here?" he answered, not moving a muscle.

"Two hundred dollars. It's all I have, Dan. I swear."

She held her hand to her chest and wept violently.

"Leave me alone, Dan. Just go. There's nothing else I can do for you. You've got all my money."

"So you liked it a lot better last night…" said Dan.

He shook his head.

"Me too," he said. "Last night you sure would have let me stay if I'd asked."

"If I were a decent sort," he continued, "I'd start over again like it was yesterday. And I'd make up for these two hundred bucks. But now I have no desire. Yesterday was just to verify something, and that's all. But yesterday left me with nothing."

"Shut up, Dan. You're a brute."

He shook his head. He seemed to be a bit astonished.

"That's what you all say. You, the regulars at Nick's, the papers. I do an honest job. It's not my fault if my brother could-

n't do the same, or you for that matter. *Last night you should have made me pay you. You shouldn't leave me believing that I can ask you for something. I need this money. If I had been able to stay with you, to know what Sheila was up to… But no, you didn't want that. Now I'm forced to do what I'm doing. And now I'll start over again… That is if the same thing can happen twice."*

Muriel looked at him, petrified by his low, monotone voice.

"They're going to ask me how I became white," he continued. *"They'll interrogate me, smash my face in, reduce me to nothing. What'll Sheila do while all this is happening? You know that I can't just let her go without keeping an eye on her."*

He looked up.

"You shouldn't call the police when I leave. Wait at least two hours."

She made an effort to look him in the eyes, but had to turn away.

She then looked at him once more, gasping for breath. He lifted his hand to strike her and she let out a strident cry. Dan's knotted-up fist crashed into her chin and she was literally lifted right off the floor. She fell back onto the bed with a muffled groan.

Dan looked at his fist. One of the joints in his hand immediately started to swell. He was astonished, and he looked at Muriel, who seemed to be sleeping. She was no longer moving and her neck was twisted at such an unnatural angle that he hoped, in spite of it all, to see her move and change positions.

He listened. Nothing outside. Muriel's scream hadn't provoked the least bit of concern from anybody.

He leaned over her and placed his weighty palm on the sheer and brilliant fabric of her bra. She was dead.

"I didn't want this…" he murmured. *"I only wanted you to keep quiet while I made my break."*

He stared down at her inert corpse. She had been quite a

beautiful girl. Really pretty for a whore.

He turned away from her and went through the handbag that was on the dresser. Twelve dollars and a bit of loose change. He took it and left, closing the two doors behind him. He locked the door and slipped the key into his pocket.

XXII

"His case is really nothing spectacular," said Cooper. "Here's what we have on him so far. He killed a prostitute, one of the regulars at the establishment where he was employed. He took her money and probably murdered her in order to rape her, given the position of the body and certain marks on the cadaver. The doctors will sort it all out and inform us. Then, he took a taxi to Brooklyn, where we lost track of him. It's been three days now that we've been on his trail and we have no idea what's become of him."

"I don't want to stay at the hotel forever," said Sheila. "And I simply can't live with the idea of going back home after all that's happened. Would you like another whiskey?"

He served himself and Sheila lit a cigarette.

"I want to live," she said. "I really loved Dan. But this man is no longer the Dan that I loved. I keep asking myself how he could have done these horrible things."

"He's got black blood," said Cooper. "That in and of itself explains a lot of things."

"Still, even now, I can't believe it," said Sheila. "In the beginning, when I learned the truth, I was so stunned that I accepted it. But now, when I start to reflect on the whole thing over again, I just can't believe it."

"All the same," said Cooper. "The civil documents are irrefutable."

"I'm completely lost," said Sheila. "I don't know what to do

or who to confide in. And in spite of everything, I still think about Dan, about what and who he was before all this."

Cooper gestured to her.

"Look, you've got to let this go," he said. "Turn the page. The past is the past. You can't dwell on it."

"I know that," said Sheila. "But it's like I'm a part of it."

She stopped for an instant.

"All this is very tough for me," she concluded. "Morally as well as physically."

"Time will help heal the wounds," said Cooper.

"I don't know," said Sheila. "I hope so."

He got up.

"It was horrible, yesterday," she said. "I wanted this whole mess to be over with. Is it really necessary, all these journalists?"

"It would seem so," said Cooper.

There was a long silence, as if he were hesitating to say something else.

"Do you think I could take you out one of these evenings?" he finally asked, almost blushing.

"That's very sweet of you," she replied with an uncertain smile.

"Not at all," he affirmed, seriously. "The pleasure would be all mine."

She sighed.

"It's funny. I never imagined that there were policemen like you."

"I take that as a compliment," said Cooper, blushing once more. "Please excuse me now, but I've got to leave. I'm on duty."

"Call me," she said.

XXIII

Dan waited. For three days now he hadn't left the filthy little room that the hotel owner, a mulatto, had been persuaded to rent to him for thirty dollars a day.

It was another dive that he had learned about at Nick's, a tip from some drunk. The bed was tough and noisy and there were cockroaches in the tiny cubbyhole that the manager had christened the "toilet."

Newspapers were piled up on the bed, the chair, all over the room.

Dan could hear the owner. He paid close attention to any noise in the building and his eyes were glued to the frame of the room's sole window, through which he could watch over the street.

Sweat rolled down his forehead. His collar was dirty and his unshaven face gave way to the shadows in the hollows of his cheeks.

XXIV

It was only five o'clock. Through the window I could see that he was alone. I had no intention of letting that disgusting worm corner me. I heard the sound of his feet in the stairwell, and then he entered his room on the second floor.

I thought of Sheila. I needed Sheila.

What else was there to think about? I laughed to myself, remembering the night when I was lying beside her, unable to do anything, and the following night when it almost happened again.

This had all taken place because of Richard. The entire fabric of my life had been turned inside out because of him.

I could hear the boss and his wife talking below. As he spoke, she tended to interrupt him, in a more or less hostile manner. She had a deep and grave tone to her voice. She was a mulatto, like him, but much darker. Thinking about her made me need Sheila all the more.

Despite my satisfaction at having killed off Richard, I knew

I had to stay cautious and wait for everything to cool down. I had to stay hidden, at all costs, and after a while the story would die down a bit and I could find Sheila and we could make our way to another country. I could, of course, leave without her, and then write later, telling her where to join me. But I just couldn't wait that long. I had about ninety-five dollars stashed, more or less, but tomorrow I had to leave the hotel. I had to go get that money one way or another.

The downstairs door squeaked and the woman said something. Her voice echoed in the staircase and her feet made their way up the steps with heavy thuds.

"There's something else in the paper," she said, waving to me from afar. "You're gonna have to go."

"Why didn't you call the cops?" I asked.

"You have to leave," she repeated. "We didn't say anything because they descended on you like a pack of wild dogs. Even if you're a vile man we know we have to help out our brothers. But now it's impossible."

"Why?" I asked. "You're afraid I'll continue like this?"

"We're not afraid," she said, "but you've got to go."

"I've paid through tomorrow."

"That doesn't make any difference," she said. "Some people claim that your brother threatened you, but that woman you killed didn't threaten you, and what's more you took her money after you raped and killed her."

I started to laugh. Raped and killed. Of course, since I was a nigger.

"Listen," I said. "You know what they write about blacks in this country. I didn't kill her. I just hit her so that she'd shut up."

She stared back at me, anxious.

"I've been here for three days," I said. "If you were running even the slightest risk you'd have been found out by now."

I was getting nervous. She spoke without any emotion, as

if anything I could have told her meant nothing more than any other mundane talk.

"Fine," I said. "I'll leave tomorrow evening, as planned. Naturally, I suggest you don't try anything."

I must have raised my voice a bit too loudly because I could now hear her husband coming up the steps.

"Don't you find it a bit steep?" I continued. "Thirty bucks a day for this disgusting room?"

"It's not about the room," she murmured. "We're sticking our necks out for your life and your freedom. My man doesn't even want you here."

The husband walked in right then. He avoided any eye contact and remained about a step behind his wife.

"Let me see that paper," I said.

"Listen to me," he said. "We've done all we can, buddy. Things are starting to get hot around here and it's just not safe. Not safe at all. So listen pal, you've got to leave this hotel."

I approached the both of them. She didn't flinch, but he slowly moved back.

"I'd like to see that paper," I said.

All of a sudden I really needed to see it. There must be something in there about my wife. The boss took a step forward, ripped the paper from his wife's hands, and then moved back towards the door.

"Get outta here and you'll find all the papers you like. And listen pal, I'd be happy to give you back that money you paid for tomorrow."

I calculated just how much force I had left. He hadn't yet tasted the fruits of my reflexes. He tried to jump back, but I already had a hold of him. I pulled him into the room and kicked the door shut.

"Give me the paper."

His wife stood motionless. Her eyes bulged as she stared at me and her two fists were pressed tight against her chest while she gasped for air.

"Give it…" I repeated with my eyes fixed straight at her.

She grabbed the paper and handed it over. I shoved it in my pocket.

"Take the cord from the curtains."

Without saying a word, she followed my orders and ripped loose the little braided strap. The man wasn't moving at all. He was frightened to death. I balled up my left hand into a fist and held it under his nose.

"Look," I said. "This is what they mean by killing a woman."

His chin cracked lightly and he went limp in my arms. I hadn't hit him too hard. This time I was sure of it. His heart was beating regularly.

"Don't be afraid," I said to his wife.

"I'm not afraid," she replied. "I did what I had to do."

I tied up his hands and shoved him under the bed.

"I'm going to step out," I said. "Just long enough to look at this paper."

I now felt calm and distant, and I unfolded the paper with steady hands. There was a report on the witnesses' statements. They all made me out to be a dangerous madman, without saying too much about me being black.

Then it spoke of Sheila. She had entrusted her business to an attorney and had started divorce proceedings.

I reread the passage two times. There wasn't even a photo. Someone was stopping certain details from getting through.

I must have spent a good long spell thinking it all over. The woman remained motionless and her husband, tucked under the bed, was also immobile.

"Do you want to eat something before you leave?"

Sheila. Those two nights. Anne, Sally, and Rosie. I hadn't touched a woman in four days. I once again pictured Muriel's body in that nylon suit she was wearing.

"No," I said. "I can't."

She noticed how I was looking at her but she said nothing. Her bosom was heaving rapidly.

I took her right on the iron bed, not even bothering to undress. She didn't make the slightest move to stop me. I was overtaken by a strange desire and I felt that an entire century had just swept past while she seemingly pulled herself out of her torpor. Her cunt was tender and burning, like the torrid force of a hot spring, and her body moved about slowly while her hands ran themselves along the length of my stiff and anxious frame. She then pressed her body up against mine. She seemed to want to imbed her flesh within mine and she moaned and grumbled like a beast, almost imperceptibly, without understanding.

XXV

I remained there for quite a while, stretched out alongside her. She made no attempt to move away. I lifted her dress up high and unconsciously ran my hands over her hard and naked belly. Then I heard the guy under the bed. He was beginning to groan and fidget. I got up. I straightened out my clothes and looked to see if the cords were still holding tight. They seemed fine. The woman then got out of bed herself.

"You have to go now," she said. "You have to."

"Listen," I said. "Just where do you want me to go?"

"You found this place," she muttered. "You'll find another…"

"They're looking for me," I said. "All over the city. I can't take a step outside without running the risk that someone recognizes me."

"I can't keep you here," she said in a low voice.

The man was moving around more forcefully under the bed. I moved over and yanked him out of his hiding place. "Where can we put him?" I asked.

She stared at me without saying a word, but the look on my face was evidently enough to persuade her because she turned around, opened the door, and led me down the staircase. We came to the first floor. There was nobody. The building was completely silent.

She had me enter a little room and then pointed to a second door that she proceeded to open. It was a rather filthy kitchen with a huge sink and a cabinet over it. It was filled with loads of crap - old brushes, jars of jam, rags.

I fashioned a sort of gag from a piece of cloth and attached it around the man's mouth, not too tightly. Then I shoved him harshly into the cabinet and closed the door, making sure that enough air could pass through the cracks in the panels.

I heard him squirm around in the cabinet. He must have been searching for the most comfortable position he could manage to find.

The woman, standing in the kitchen, was once again motionless.

"Listen," I said. "Do you hear me?"

She nodded.

"You're going to go to this address. You're going to ask if Mrs. Parker is still there. Sheila Parker. My wife."

She once again nodded her head as a sign of acceptance.

"If she's not there then try to find out where she is and where the baby is."

"Is he your son?" she said.

I nodded back at her without saying anything. I felt my throat tighten.

There was a moment of silence.

"I'll leave after that," I said. "But I have to know."

I gave her the address and a few details. She quietly left the room and I heard her close the other door. I looked around. I finally located a piece of soap and a razor, and then quickly cleaned myself up in front of a much too tiny mirror. I found a few things to eat in the icebox.

I had one hell of an appetite.

XXVI

By the time the woman had come back it was pitch black outside. I had settled down in the woman's room and every now and then would go and see if my lodger wasn't suffering too much in his cabinet.

I was almost happy when I saw her coming back, yet a terrible anguish made me fear the news she had in store for me.

She came in. I heard her steps in the other room and she went to check the kitchen. She then came back to her bedroom and showed absolutely no surprise at the fact that I had settled into her digs.

"She left," she said. "She's at the Welcome Hotel, not far away. The kid is at his grandmother's. But your wife's fine; she's planning to come back home soon, probably in two or three days. Maybe before that."

"You spoke with her?" I asked.

"The maids at the hotel told me."

"How do they know?"

She smiled, but it wasn't a cheerful smile.

"They have ears. She talked about this stuff with one of the cops. Cooper's his name. He's been quite attentive towards her. They all tease him about it at the hotel. He blushes like a little girl. It's a small hotel."

"Is there a lot of surveillance?" I asked.

"A few cops," she said. "Not too many. It's really the

papers that have made a big deal out of it. The fact of the matter is that it's just some nigger and a couple of whores who got snuffed, and that really doesn't bother the police or people in general. The whole murder and rape story played well in the papers. It'll play well in the courts, too. But nobody's really that obsessed with it."

"Why are you talking about the courts?" I asked bluntly.

"You're going to screw up because of this woman," she said. "You had the time get out of here, to hide yourself away, but you've let them trap you. Now they're just waiting for you to throw yourself at their feet."

I laughed, cynically.

"Well they can hope all they want that I end up in front of a judge," I said. "It's no sweat off their backs."

She casually began to undress.

"What are you doing?" I asked.

She stopped and said, "I'm going to bed. I don't think you'll be able to relax if I try to sleep somewhere else. I've got no intention of turning you in. I don't think that you're dangerous."

She walked past me and stretched out on the bed.

"You can get under the sheets," I told her. "I don't feel like another go around."

She said nothing and slid under the covers. I went to close the curtains and I turned on a light. All of a sudden I was disgusted by the room and its odor. I had to fight to keep myself from vomiting. I needed some alcohol.

I went into the other room, which obviously served as some sort of office. I found something to drink in the cupboard. A cheap bottle of rum.

It was half-full. Enough to put me to sleep.

I closed the door that looked out onto the staircase and then put the key in my pocket.

I would have paid a pretty penny to have a revolver

right now.

I came back to the room with the bottle. I sat down on a chair next to the table and started to drink. It was vile.

I had one more chance to see Sheila, at her hotel, before she left. I got up. I checked the cabinet. Coming back, I passed by the window and pulled back the curtain to get a glimpse outside. I caught a quick glimpse of a car rounding the corner. A police car.

I tried to see if anyone had gotten out. They would have been in front of the hotel. I pressed my face to the window.

I heard someone knocking on the door downstairs and ringing the bell.

I immediately made for the staircase. I closed the door behind me and locked the deadbolts, then slipped the key into my pocket. I moved up quickly and within a minute I'd reached the top floor. Once up there, I located the attic window and crawled out onto the roof. There wasn't a moment to lose. Obviously, they were hoping to corner me in my room.

If I was swift enough, and if I could mange to find a way out, I'd have the time to stop by Sheila's.

I crept over the rooftop until I reached the neighboring building, which was at least four stories lower than where I was standing. I ran as quickly as I could, but it was a real steep fall.

I could hear some sort of commotion below me and I felt myself grinding my teeth, trying to stay calm. I had reached the hotel's interior courtyard and was now right next to the edge of the neighboring building.

There was nothing to hang on to.

I moved towards the street, and slowly, without a sound, I looked over the edge.

There were four men waiting down on the street. Cops. I could recognize their hats. They didn't see me.

I had the choice between shimmying up a pipe or taking

the ladder that was bolted into the wall. The ladder was in a sorry state. I didn't dare risk it.

Still, sliding up that pipe seemed impossible. I grabbed hold of the first of the ladder's U-shaped rungs. It was corroded with rust and broke away from my hand.

There was one other means of escape. I took advantage of the space I had created and slid behind the rungs of the U-shaped ladder. This way, I could climb up with my back to the building. But I was a prisoner inside a cage of rungs. I ascended as rapidly as possible.

They must have been wasting time trying to kick in those two doors of the hotel. When I reached the eleventh rung it also gave way and I had to stabilize myself with my knees and my elbows.

With my last bit of force, I finally reached the top of the neighboring building. I turned myself around and pulled my body up over the ledge. At that very moment, there was a violent shock and bits of stone rained down onto my right hand.

I didn't waste any time. I moved quickly over the roof. It was quite a steep slope, but I managed to keep myself upright. And I ran - yes, ran – over the grayish metal. I didn't bother looking to the right or to the left. My eyes were simply fixed on the next rooftop. I had to shake off the cops, and do so as quickly as possible.

The next building was exactly the same height as the one I was now on. I kept running, weaving a wild and clumsy path that forced my body to writhe and twist in hideous terror in order to keep my balance.

The roof of the next building represented a drop of about two yards, but its slope, even steeper, stopped me as I slid to the edge. I turned and held on. I fought and scraped with my feet until I reached the rooftop. I moved about four feet over to a chimney, and once there, I could make out a glass-covered opening of sufficiently large dimensions.

I stuck to the roof like a leech and headed for the window. My eyes greedily peered inside.

Not a soul.

I covered my right hand with the end of my sleeve and smashed through the window with a single blow. I swiftly made a wider opening and slipped inside.

There were some clothes in a closet. I quickly exchanged my blue jacket for a gray one, not forgetting to empty the pockets of my old garment. The gray one fit, more or less. I also grabbed a new hat and then made for the door. It was locked from the outside. I turned the inside bolt and it opened. I left.

I stopped at the landing of the staircase. Nobody. There was a stir of voices from below. I pricked up my ears and realized that half of the people were outside, obsessed with the manhunt – the hunt for me.

I walked down silently. Nobody paid attention. At first, I moved along with the crowd and then I slowly started to break away.

I turned down the next street.

There were some cigarettes in the gray jacket. I took one out and lit it, wanting to appear casual.

They had a whole night ahead of them to spend searching through houses.

Plenty of time to pay a little visit to Sheila.

My loins and my muscles were aching something terrible, but I felt free - more free than I had ever felt.

I remembered the dull thud of the bullet grazing my hand. I looked at it. There was a little scratch, a mark of dried blood. I sucked at the tiny little wound and suddenly realized that I needed a revolver.

I still had enough dough to buy one, used, at a pawnshop.

I knew that there was a place not far from where I was. Not far from Sheila's either. The owner was an old guy, and he had plenty of money.

I was still leery about taking the subway. A taxi would be less risky.

I hailed the first cab that came by and gave him the address. The real, exact address. No need to get worried at this stage. The time to worry is when there's real danger. Big danger. A taxi driver just didn't represent any real threat.

After I got out and paid, I realized that the store was closed. No matter. I knew the old man lived behind his shop. I just had to go around to the other side.

I walked into the building and rang the doorbell. He rushed to the door and opened it just a crack in order to peer outside. The chain was long enough for me to slip my foot into the opening. I grabbed him by the lapel of his crumpled old suit and threatened him with something.

"Open up," I said, "or I'll fire. Be quick about it and you won't get hurt."

His hands fumbled around for the chain. I could hear his labored breathing.

I walked in.

"Hey," I said, letting go of him. "You recognize me?"

"But…. huh…" he was just murmuring, still terrified.

"Yeah, it's Dan." I said. "I want to buy a revolver. And some cartridges."

"You? But you've already got one," he muttered.

"No I don't," I said.

I handed him the key that I had fooled him into believing was a gun.

"Keep it as a souvenir," I said. "And hurry up."

He didn't seem too reassured. I followed him into his shop.

"But if I sell you a gun," he objected, "I'll wind up in the can myself."

"It'll be fine," I said. "We'll cook up some bogus story. Get going. And step on it."

He opened the drawer under his counter. There was a diverse array of weapons. I grabbed a big one and checked out the chamber. It wasn't loaded.

"Shells," I said.

He passed me a small box of cartridges and I loaded the gun. I put the remainder in my pocket, but the revolver was really too heavy to carry there. I'd have to slip it under my belt. Then I changed my mind. I brazenly took aim at the old man.

"You don't happen to have a little cash around here?" I asked.

He didn't say a word. He just held up his hands. His mouth was twitching as if he were a nervous little rabbit.

"No, don't do that," I said. "Drop your hands. That's trust for you. You know very well that I kill with my fists."

He obeyed and then rummaged through his pockets. He pulled out a fat old wallet and handed it over.

"Only the money," I said. "No checks."

He started to cry. It was a lot of money.

"Your daily receipts?" I remarked. "Business is good. They buy as much as they pawn, and you profit either way."

I grabbed the bills and shoved them into my jacket.

"You wouldn't also happen to have a nice little suit in my size, would you? Something the ladies would like?"

Without uttering a word, he moved towards the rear of the store and pointed to some clothes hanging on a few hooks. I took a pinstriped, chestnut-colored suit, not too flashy, but different enough from the one I was wearing.

I was standing behind him and I tapped him lightly on the head with the butt of my .38. He was now lying on the floor. I took my time changing and went to the back of the shop to get cleaned up. I felt a lot better.

I came back into the shop and let out a sigh of regret when I saw the telephone. It would have been so simple to have met with Sheila at the train station and simply left with her.

I remembered that article in the paper. Divorce proceedings. First there was that. Second, the line to the hotel must be tapped.

I sighed. The old man was still stretched out on the ground. It all left me feeling more and more numb. I'd been killing people for two days now, and for the five years that proceeded that I had been dishing out beatings. There wasn't much difference.

Anyway, this guy wasn't dead yet. In order to make sure of it I just had to set the shop on fire. It would serve the purpose of shifting the cops' attention away from the hotel where I wanted to go. Plus, it would give them and the firemen a chance to get a bit of exercise.

I found some gasoline. Why not? There was just about everything in that little shop. I accumulated about all I could in terms of combustible old crap and dumped it right in the middle of the place. I stacked up a bunch of furniture, clothing, paper, wood, tires, and just about anything else I could find, then showered it with gasoline.

I tossed a match onto the pile. At first, it seemed to extinguish itself, and then suddenly there was a huge "poof" and the flames of the fire licked my face. I quickly made my way through the back of the shop, down the hallway, and quietly stepped outside. The fire roared and crackled and raged. I left the building and walked back up the street, never bothering to look back.

I arrived in front of the hotel just at the moment when the robust fire engines were crossing the intersection with an infernal blare. All of a sudden I felt really tired, and then, just as quickly, the feeling dissipated. People came to look out their doors and windows, and the more nosey citizens in the crowd started following the trucks to the scene of the arson. The alarm must have been sounded right away.

It was more of a residential hotel than a tourist's place. Not very big. It seemed cozy enough. A couple of waiters appeared on the doorstep. They paid me no mind. There was a restaurant downstairs and I pushed my way through the revolving door. I could feel the contact of the long, hard panels as they pressed up against my hips and abdomen.

I made a short stop in the men's room, then headed back up the stairs, cutting through the hallway that in all likelihood led to the lobby.

I knew enough about the layout of bars, restaurants, and other public places, so I wasn't worried about losing my way.

The attendant was yawning in front of the elevator. I slipped him a ten-dollar bill.

"Take me up to Mrs. Parker's room, quick. Then go back down and find me some flowers," I said. "Get a move on."

He quickly shoved the bill into his pocket and closed the doors. He had hardly even looked at me.

"The blonde lady?" he asked, just to make sure.

"That's right," I said. "The blonde. I'm her cousin."

He grinned a sheepish grin.

XVII

The old man was still breathing. The right side of his body was hideously burned, and his charred clothing stuck to his bloody flesh. His right hand was shaking and a non-stop succession of incoherent words flowed from his lips.

Two men cautiously lifted him up, straddling the blackened flesh that was still smoking and covered with puss. They carved a path through the rubble.

The fire had ravaged the upper floors of the building and the roar of the motors was competing with that of the flames.

They carefully placed him into the ambulance. The old

man seized the sleeve of one of the ambulance attendants.

"A cop..." he murmured. "Get me a cop..."

"Sure," said the nurse. "But just calm down. We'll be there in a minute."

His eyes, with their blackened lashes, suddenly popped half-open and he stared at the nurse. The latter turned away so that he wouldn't have to look at the bloody sheen of the man's eyelids and the pain-stricken grimace on his face.

"Dan..." he said. "Dan Parker...It was him... the fire..."

The nurse jumped to his feet.

"Wait!" He was shouting at the driver of the car that was getting ready to pull away.

He ran towards a cop. The crowd, greedily fixated on the spectacle at hand, scurried around behind the police blockade.

"Hey!" shouted the nurse. "I've got some new news for you guys. Get over here, quick!"

The cop followed him.

"Seems Dan Parker had a hand in this," said the nurse, almost out of breath. "The old man told me. Most people around here consider him a bit of a nut, but all the same..."

The cop moved over towards the wounded man. A few yards away, a chunk of wall tore loose and came crumbling down with an incredible roar.

"You're telling me it was Dan Parker?" asked the officer.

The old man's eyes were now closed again. He made a vague gesture with his head.

"He took a .38... and a suit... brown, pinstriped..." He could barely speak. "He went to see a woman... and my money... I've gotta get my money back... It was Dan Parker... all my money..."

The cop paid close attention to his words.

"Where did he go?" asked the officer. "Do you know?"

"He beat me," said the old man. "My head... My money...brown suit...went to see a woman..."

"What woman?" insisted the officer.

The old man's head was rolling around from left to right.

"Listen," said the nurse. "We've got to get going, or else he'll bite it right here."

"I'll meet you at the hospital," said the cop.

The Herculean ambulance sped away like the wind.

XVIII

Crane smashed his fist against the table.

"He slipped right through our fingers," he said. "Nothing we can do now. There's no way out of this problem. They scoured through the first three buildings from top to bottom. They've almost finished with the fourth, and of course, they won't find a thing."

He stopped talking. The telephone was ringing. He answered, listened, responded in monosyllabic fashion, and then hung up.

"They've finished," he said. "Nothing. His hat and coat were in one of the upstairs rooms of the fourth building. He just had to slip down the stairs. Still, it was impressive!"

He pounded on the desktop again and all his files went flying.

"And just what did you tell me a little earlier?" he blurted. "That this guy isn't any more black than you or me?"

Cooper shook his head. He felt uncomfortable.

"It's just a fact and we can't do anything about it. We made a mistake."

"Well I don't give damn! Why did we screw up? How does this make us look? We were stupid not to have seen all this from the start. This is going to cause one hell of a stink, even bigger than before, and they'll be waiting for our next move. What'll it look like? The papers have been all over this for four days, over every last detail, and they keep harping on this

business about marriage and divorce between Blacks and Whites. And this is the news you bring me? That this guy is white! I mean really, for Christ's sake, just what makes this guy white, after all?"

"It's not my fault," said Cooper. "I'll be the first to admit that I regret how things turned out. But he panicked. Sure, we could have stopped the second murder and this whole sordid story. And it's true that he's saved his neck this time. What's more, a good lawyer could have had him acquitted. Then there's this guy Richard, a master blackmailer. And Dan himself believes that he's Black, and had I not by coincidence stumbled onto the information I gave you nobody would have known that he's white."

"Jesus fucking Christ Almighty!" said Crane, red with rage. There was a moment of silence. The telephone rang again.

"Yeah," shouted Crane into the telephone.

He kept his ear to the receiver for a couple of moments.

"Where?" he barked. "There? Over where the woman is?"

Cooper turned red and looked away. Crane put down the receiver and stood up.

"Get a move on!" he said. "Dan just set fire to a pawnbroker's shop some five minutes away from his wife's hotel room. He knocked out the old man and then left in a brown pinstriped suit. Get going! What are you waiting for? Take as many officers as you need."

Cooper got up and headed to the door. Crane followed him.

"And try to stop him from killing anybody else," said Crane. "Better to shoot first and ask questions later."

Cooper stared back at him and then lowered his eyes. Crane laughed, cynically.

"You'll feel a lot calmer afterwards."

Cooper had to fight to hold back his impulses. He turned and walked down the hallway. Crane kicked the door shut. He grumbled something to himself and sat back down at his desk.

XXIX

Dan stopped in the hallway. He turned around and watched the elevator door close behind him. He looked to the right, then to the left, and with an almost unconscious gesture tried to flatten out the bulge at his waistline that was accentuated by the butt of his revolver.

The woman at the hotel had given him Sheila's room number. It was the third door down. He looked back, furtively glancing over his shoulder, and then gently, with the utmost precaution, he turned the handle and tugged at the door. But the door held firm. He started pulling harder and had almost lost his composure when he suddenly realized that the door opened in the other direction. He entered.

The room was furnished very plainly. The windows were covered by two long curtains, which Dan automatically recognized as a possible hiding place. The window was open and the streets were all ablaze with bright lights.

There was a bed, two armchairs, a table and some cupboards. There was also a little door. The bathroom, no doubt.

Dan listened attentively. It was completely silent. Nobody in the bathroom. He moved towards the door and then heard the sounds of footsteps coming down the hallway. Not much time. He moved back to the window and hid himself behind one of the curtains.

Sheila walked in. She must have come from somewhere else on the same floor. Dan wasn't able to see her. Through the open door he could hear the noise of the elevator and the voice of the attendant who was calling out to Sheila. She stopped. The elevator attendant handed her some flowers and she thanked him. The door was now closed. The elevator operator had mentioned something to her about some guy, big and strong, wearing a chestnut-colored suit. Sheila didn't seem to have any idea who it might be. The attendant seemed to be on familiar terms with Sheila, and she didn't seem surprised by his message.

She walked around for a bit and then headed over to the bathroom. Dan could hear the sound of water filling up a vase and the little thud that came when she placed it on the table. She took off her shoes and put on some slippers.

There was a moment of silence. Dan didn't dare reveal himself. He now felt afraid that his presence would terrify her. Still, the waiting started to feel interminable to him.

In the distance there was the blare of a police siren. It seemed to be getting closer. Cautiously, Dan turned around and through the window he could see a police car and a bunch of cops on motorcycles.

The police car came to a stop in front of the hotel. Dan's heart started pounding more forcefully, but not any more rapidly. He wasn't afraid.

Somehow, Sheila's presence put him at ease. He would have liked to stay there longer. Nothing had happened yet. Things just might just blow over. He could come out from behind the curtain and lose himself in Sheila's embrace.

One could now hear the voices of Cooper and the elevator attendant as the two of them made their way down the hall.

Cooper entered the room and closed the door behind him.

"Your husband's in the hotel," he stated bluntly. "He killed a man in a little shop nearby. He came in wearing a suit that he stole from the shop and the elevator operator recognized his photo. He isn't here, is he?"

"Here! Oh, no… This is horrible… Mr. Cooper, I'm begging you, get me out of here! My God, how terryfying… I didn't know… I've been in the bathroom and all this time he was here!"

Cooper quickly moved over to the bathroom and pulled back the plastic shower curtain.

"You would have seen him," he said. "He would have

shown himself. He must be hiding somewhere in the hotel.
Stay here and don't move. I'm going to search the hotel with
my men."

"I'm going to die of fright," mumbled Sheila.

"I don't think you have anything to fear from him," said
Cooper. "Be patient. This will all be over soon."

"Can't you stay with me?" sighed Sheila.

"No, I can't," he said. "Every minute we wait just gives
him more time to escape."

He was standing close to her, and Dan could tell that
Cooper had his arms around her shoulders.

"Now, now," said Cooper. "I'm going to tell you something
that'll help put you at ease. Your husband isn't black. I've
found papers that prove it. Yeah, he's killed three people, but a
good attorney will be able to get him a lighter sentence. He
won't go to the chair. Now will this help settle you down?"

"Not black?" she murmured. "But… I mean, didn't he kill
his brother?"

"It wasn't his brother," said Cooper. "The guy he killed was
a master blackmailer. Dan just lost his head. We can get him
out of this mess by exploiting the fact that he was driven to
murder because of these circumstances."

He stopped for a moment.

"That shouldn't stop you from divorcing him," he said.
"Anyway… it'll make matters easier."

A sound came from behind the curtains and Cooper quick-
ly turned around. He pulled out his revolver. People were
screaming down on the street. He dashed over to the window.

XXX

I couldn't move. The cop came in and I remained
behind the curtains. If he took a step in my direction I

would be forced to shoot him, and I didn't want to do that. I could only wait.

Maybe they won't find me. Maybe they'll just go away. Sheila seemed frightened. She must be holding onto the arm of that cop, just like she used to hold onto mine, a long time ago. I wanted to see her. I would have given anything just to see her. But now he was here. She was no longer alone. I might have tried peeping through the window, but now there's this cop and he's on my trail. They must be surrounding the building. The whole mess is starting over again. Everywhere I go now I'm surrounded. They're lying in wait for me like I'm some sort of wild cat stuck up in a tree.

I wasn't paying attention to what they were saying. I just heard voices, and then the words from that copper's mouth that sliced into my head like a bloody razor when he said I wasn't black.

Then I no longer saw anything at all and I came to understand what I had done. I had been afraid for so long, believing that they were pursuing me. I'd been smashing people's faces in for years, up to the point where I had grown sick of it. I was surprised to find myself at ease among them, to feel that I was just like them. I remembered what a black schoolmate of mine had said to me one day. I was proud of being white, and I asked him, "What does it feel like, being black?" I saw that he was surprised and a bit ashamed, almost crushed. He was on the verge of tears, and then he said, "It doesn't feel like anything at all, Dan, and you know it." I hit him and gave him a bloody lip. He opened his eyes and looked at me. He didn't understand.

I was really terrified at the beginning, when people started treating me like a White person. It was quite audacious of me to have taken that job at the bar. But they didn't ask any questions. Little by little everything fell into place. All

the same, I wanted to take out my revenge on them.
"They smell." That's what Whites say. But I was proud
because I didn't have that particular odor. Then again, one
doesn't smell one's own odor. Moreover, I was strong, and
I took pride in that just as I had taken pride in being
white. But then Richard came. I had spent my childhood
with him. He really was my brother. At least at that
moment I believed it – the moment I killed him. Sheila
must have believed it, too. I was so full of pride when I
married her. It was like an act of vengeance, and it was
also vengeance when I saw that I had come to fully possess
her. And so little by little I became white. It took years to
wipe away all the traces, and then all it took was for
Richard to show up and once again I found myself believing I was Black. Then came those two girls, Anne and
Sally. I would have never believed I was impotent had I
not been convinced that black blood was coursing through
my veins. Then I had to kill Richard. If I had just called
the police they would have found the papers proving that
I was white, and Richard would have left, end of story.

I killed Richard for nothing. His bones snapped under
the force of my hands. I killed the girl with one punch.
And now the pawnbroker is dead, again for no reason.
Stupid. He must have burned to death. I killed them all
for absolutely no reason. And now I've lost Sheila and the
hotel is being surrounded.

The cop said something about making matters easier.
Well, there are other ways to simplify things.

XXXI

*Dan seemed to be waking from a dream. In a movement
that was at once slow and inexorable, he stepped over the*

ledge of the window, hunching down so that he could pass through its frame. Far down below, on the pavement, he could see a densely packed crowd of people, and instinctively, he tensed up his muscles in order to avoid them. His body twisted in the air like a clumsy frog and came crashing down onto the rock-hard pavement of the street.

The assistant photographer, Max Klein, had just enough time to take the shot of his career before the police hauled away the cadaver. The photo came out in Life magazine a few days later. It was a fantastic shot.

THE DEAD ALL HAVE THE SAME SKIN

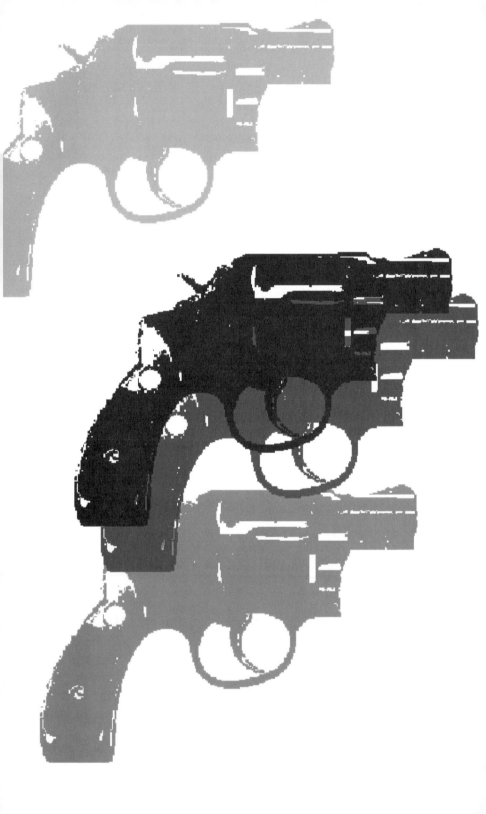

Dogs, Desire, and Death

They've got me. I'm going to the chair tomorrow. Still, I'm going to write about it. I want to explain things. The jury just didn't understand. What's more, Slacks is dead now, which has made it all the more difficult to speak about it, knowing that they wouldn't believe me. If she had only been able to free herself from the car, to come and explain it all. But let's not beat a dead dog. There's nothing more I can do now. Nothing at all.

The drag about being a taxi driver is the little routines you get into. You drive around all day and out of habit you come to know all the neighborhoods. There are some that you like better than others. I know guys who would rather be passed through a meat grinder than take a fare to Brooklyn. For me, it's no problem. I just do it - no questions asked. What I mean is that I used to do it, because now, well, I don't do it at all.

Going to The Three Deuces at one in the morning was another little habit I had. One night I brought a customer there who was dead drunk and he wanted me to come in with him. I came back out. I knew the types of girls you run into in these places. It's just stupid, really. You'd say as much yourself…

Every night, at one o'clock, give or take five minutes, I would pass by. That's when she walked out. The Three Deuces often featured a *chanteuse*, and this evening I recognized the headliner. They called her "Slacks" because she was almost always dressed in pants. In the papers, they also claimed she was a lesbian. Almost every night she would leave with the two same guys, her piano player and her bassist, and then drive away in the piano player's car. They would head off somewhere for another gig and then come back to The Three Deuces to finish up the evening. I only learned that later.

I never stayed there too long. I couldn't leave the cab unattended all the time or just parked for long periods either, and anyway there were a lot more customers in that neighborhood than almost anywhere else. However, this particular evening the three of them had some sort of argument, and it seemed to be something serious. She struck the pianist in the face, and her blow had some real force behind it. He hit the ground like he'd been belted by a cop. He was dead drunk, but I think the smack she gave him would have floored him even if he'd been completely sober, and now, plastered as he was, he couldn't manage to get back on his feet. In an attempt to rouse him back to consciousness the other guy gave him a few slaps on the face. I'll never know how things turned out because she came running over to my cab, opened the door, and slid inside, right down next to me on the front seat. Then she sparked up her lighter and stared me straight in the face.

"You want me to turn the light on inside the cab?"

She said no and then put out the flame of her lighter. I took off. After a while, when I turned on to York Avenue, I asked her for an address because I finally realized she hadn't said a word.

"Just go straight ahead."

It was all the same to me, as long as the meter was running. I just kept driving straight ahead. In the center of town, where all the clubs are, there are still people around, but once you hit the outskirts there's nothing. A bunch of empty streets. Hard to believe, but it's really even worse than the suburbs after one in the morning. Maybe a car or two, or some lone soul walking down the street.

After she got it into her head to sit down right next to me I knew that I wouldn't be in for any conventional behavior on the part of this chick. I examined her profile. She had shoulder-length black hair and her skin was so pale that she almost looked ill. Her lips were painted a blackish shade of red and it made her mouth look like a shadowy hole. We just kept moving along. Then she decided to speak.

"Let me take the wheel."

I stopped the car. I decided not to argue about it after seeing the way she took down her partner. I had no desire to get into a scuffle with a female of this caliber. I started to get out, but then she grabbed me by my arm.

"Don't bother. I'll just slide over you. Come on, move."

She climbed over my knees and slid to my left. She was really built – her body was as hard as an icebox but not quite the same temperature.

She could tell that this little maneuver had gotten me aroused and she started to laugh. But there was no meanness to it. She almost seemed happy. When she took off I thought the speedometer of my old rig was going to explode. She accelerated so brutally that our bodies plunged a good foot back into the seats.

We'd crossed the Harlem River and were coming up on the Bronx. Damn the torpedoes. She crushed that accelerator pedal like there was no tomorrow. When I was in the army I saw how those nuts drive in France, and let me tell you they really know how to destroy a car. But their little massacres weren't even a fraction of what this bitch in pants was capable of. The French are just dangerous. This broad was a catastrophe. Still, I kept my mouth shut.

So you find this funny, hey? You think that with my size and my muscle I should have been able to handle this female. Well, you wouldn't have dared touch her either if you could have seen her mouth and the look on her face in that car. White as a cadaver, and that black hole... I glanced over at her, still silent, and tried to look around at the same time. I wouldn't have wanted a cop to nail the both of us.

You wouldn't think it, but I'm telling you that in a city like New York there aren't a whole hell of a lot of people wandering around after a certain hour. She'd just turn whenever she felt like it, down any street. We'd pass block after block without seeing a single soul, and then every so often we'd catch a glimpse of one or two people - maybe a bum, sometimes a woman, people coming home from work. There are also stores that stay open till one or two in the morning, and even some that never close. Every time she'd see a guy on the sidewalk to her right she'd swing the steering wheel over and bring the car right to the edge of the curb, as close as possible to the pedestrian. Then she would slow down a little just before approaching him, and when she got right up next to the guy she'd stomp down on the accelerator pedal and speed past him. I tried to keep quiet, but after the fourth time I just had to ask.

"Why are you doing that?"

"I guess I find it amusing," she said.

I didn't have any response. She looked over at me. Under no circumstance did I want her looking at me while she was driving, and so in spite of myself I reached over and grabbed the wheel. She took her fist and smashed it against my hand. I hadn't seen it coming. It was like a horse stomping on my knuckles. I cursed, and she started to laugh again.

"It's a riot, the way they jump up in the air the minute they hear the motor roar!"

She surely saw the dog that was crossing the street up ahead, so I tried to find something to grab onto to prepare myself for the blow of her slamming on the brakes. But instead of slowing down, she accelerated, and I heard a heavy thud come from the front of the car and felt the shock.

"Jesus!" I said. "You're really pushing it! Taking out a dog like that could have totaled this car…"

"Shut up!"

She looked like she was in a daze. She had a faraway look in her eyes and the car wasn't rolling real straight. After a couple of blocks she pulled over.

I wanted to get out and see if she'd screwed up the radiator, but she grabbed me by the arm. She was panting like a racehorse.

Her face at just that moment was something that I'll never be able to forget. To see a woman in that state is fine when it's you yourself who's put her there. That's great. But I was miles away from even entertaining those thoughts. And now to see her all of the sudden like that… She remained motionless and squeezed my wrist with all her might. And she was drooling a bit. The corners of her mouth were all wet.

I looked outside. I couldn't tell where we were. There wasn't a soul around. Her pants came off with one tug at the zipper. In a car, it usually isn't very satisfying. Still, in spite of that, this was one experience I won't be likely to forget. Even when those boys come to shave my head tomorrow morning.

***

Shortly thereafter, I had her slide back over to the right and I was once again at the wheel. But she made me stop the car almost immediately. She got herself cleaned up as best she could, swearing like a soldier the whole time, and then stepped out and climbed into the back seat. She gave me the address of a nightclub where she had to go and sing and I tried to remember just where we were. My mind was cloudy, like that of someone who regains consciousness after a month in a hospital. I nevertheless succeeded in getting up on my own two feet to go take a look at the front of the car. No harm done – just a spot of blood that had spread out over the right fender due to the speed of the wind hitting it. It could have been anything.

I did the quickest thing: made a simple u-turn and followed the same path back.

I could see her in my rearview mirror. She looked out the window as we drove, and as we passed by the dog's carcass, now lying on the sidewalk, I could hear her. Once again she started to breathe heavily. The dog's body was still trembling; the crash must have ruptured its kidneys and all it was able to do was drag itself to the edge of the street. I felt weak and wanted to vomit, and behind me I could hear her start to laugh. She knew I was sick and she started to poke fun at me, saying horrible things. Still, I could have taken her again, right there in the middle of the street.

Well, boys, I don't know what kind of stuff you're made of, but after I dropped her back at the club where she was supposed to do her number I just didn't have it in me to wait around for her. I took off right away. I had to get back home, to get some sleep. It's not always a ball living alone, but Jesus Christ was I ever happy to be alone at the end of that evening. I didn't even bother to undress. I just grabbed something to drink and threw myself onto my bed, completely emptied. Christ, was I ever wiped out...

Then, the very next night, I was back for more, waiting for her right out in front. I lit up my on-duty light and took a few steps towards the pavement. It's a real busy little part of town. I knew I couldn't just wait around, but I did so all the same. She came out right at the same time - regular as a stopwatch, this girl. She saw me right away and had no problem recognizing me. Her pals were in tow, as usual, and she was laughing that special little laugh of hers. I don't know just how to explain it to you, but seeing her like that suddenly made me feel like my feet had left the ground. She opened the door to the taxi and all three of them slid in. I felt suffocated – a reaction that surprised me. "You're a fool," I thought to myself. A woman like that always operates at the mercy of her whims. One night, you're some great guy, and the next, your just another taxi driver, another nobody.

That's right!... Just another nobody... I was driving like an idiot and almost smashed into the rear-end of a huge car right in front of me. Sure, I was angry, now that I was of no use to her anymore. I could hear the three of them joking around in back. She was telling stories with that mannish voice of hers. That voice... good God... The way it exploded out of her throat all backwards and twisted left me feeling intoxicated.

As soon as we hit our destination she was the first to step out. The other two made no attempt to pay – they knew her well enough. They went into the club and she came over and leaned through the window, giving me a little peck on the cheek as if I were a baby. I took her money. I didn't want any trouble with her. I was about to say something. I was looking for just the right words, but she spoke first.

"Will you wait for me?" she asked.

"Where?"

"Here. I'll be back in fifteen minutes." "Alone?"

Christ, was I ever full of myself. I wished I could have taken that back, but it was too late. She dug her nails into my cheek.

"See what you get?" she said.

She laughed again. As for me, I was just dumbfounded. She let go of me almost immediately and I sat there, blood dripping from the spot where she'd grabbed me.

"It's nothing!" she said. "You'll have stopped bleeding by the time I get back. Now you're going to wait for me, understood? Right here."

She walked into the club. I tried to get a glimpse of her in the rearview mirror. I had three scratch marks running along my cheek and a fourth mark, even bigger, right in the middle of my face. Her thumb. It wasn't bleeding too badly. Anyway, I couldn't feel a thing.

So I just sat there, waiting. We didn't kill anything that night. And I didn't see any action, either.

***

I don't think it's something she'd been doing for long, this little number of ours. She didn't speak much and I knew absolutely nothing about her. I was now keeping a low profile during the day and then at night I'd go pick her up in my old wreck of a cab. She didn't sit next to me any more – it would have been a pain in the ass to get busted for that. I would just get out and she'd take my place. Usually two or three times a week we'd manage to run down a dog or a cat.

Towards the second month of our relationship, I got the feeling that she was getting hungry for something new. She just wasn't getting off like at first and I think she'd convinced herself that it was time to set our sights on bigger game. There's not much more I can tell you. I just found it natural. She wasn't getting the desired reaction, and I wanted it to be like it was before. Sure, you think I'm a monster. But you've never met this girl. It didn't matter if was a dog or a little kid. I would have killed anything for her. And so one evening we did. We killed a fifteen year-old girl who was out walking with her boyfriend, a sailor. She was coming back from an amusement park. Let me tell you about it.

Slacks was a terror on that particular evening. As soon as

she got in I could see she really wanted it. We would definite-
ly have to find something, even if that meant driving all night.

Jesus, did things get off to a bad start. I headed straight
for Queensborough Bridge and then onto the freeway.
Never in my life had I seen so many cars and so few pedes-
trians. Well, you might say, that's normal, being that it's a
freeway. But I just didn't feel it that night. I couldn't get it
working. We drove for miles and miles. We made a complete circle and ended up at Coney Island. Slacks had taken
the wheel just a couple of minutes earlier. I was in back, trying to steady myself in response to her sudden turns. She
looked insane. As usual, I simply waited. I was almost
asleep, you understand, but I came to again in the back seat
when we finally passed by our victim. Hell, I don't even
want to think about it.

It was quite simple, really. Slacks was zigzagging between
24th west and 23rd street when she saw them. They were
having a good time, him walking on the pavement with her
at his side, in the street, making it look like she was even
smaller than she was. He was a big, handsome boy. Looking
at her back, you could tell she was real young. She had
blonde hair and was wearing a little dress. There wasn't too
much light, but I could see Slack's hands gripping the
wheel. That bitch could really drive. She smashed into
them, striking the girl in the hip. I felt like I was going to
die. As soon as I was able to turn around I could see her
lying there, a lifeless mass. The boy was screaming, chasing
after us. It was then when I saw an old, green cop car come
out of nowhere.

"Step on it!" I yelled.

She looked over at me for a second and we almost went
flying into the sidewalk.

"Faster!... Get moving!..."

I understand now something that had escaped me at that

moment. Now I know. I could no longer see anything but her back, but now I understand what was destined to happen. That's why the boys can go ahead and shave my melon tomorrow morning. I don't even care if they make a mockery of it, leave ridiculous strands running all over my face, or paint me green like the cop car. I just don't give a damn, you understand.

Slacks was really moving. She was handling the car pretty well and we ended up on Surf Avenue. My old heap was making a murderous screech. The squad car must have been right behind in hot pursuit.

We finally reached the onramp to the freeway. No more red lights. Christ, if I only had another car. It was total chaos. Plus, the other vehicle was closing in. We were racing, but at a snail's pace. It was torture - like pulling out your fingernails with your own teeth.

Slacks put all she had into it. I could still see her back and I now understood what she wanted. I shouted again: "Step on it!..." and she kept going. She turned her head for a second and some other guy came barreling after us on the same ramp. She didn't see him. He pulled up on our right. He must have been doing seventy-five miles an hour. I saw the tree coming and curled up into a little ball, but she didn't move a muscle. When they pulled me from the wreck I was screaming like a beast, but Slacks was motionless. The steering wheel had been driven straight into her chest. They had a hell of a time getting her out of there. They just kept pulling on her white arms, which were as pale as her face. She was still drooling a little. Her eyes were wide open. I couldn't move either because my foot was bent backwards under my leg in the wrong direction, but I asked them to carry me over to her. I could make out her eyes, and then I saw it all, her whole body. She was covered with blood. Rivers of blood. Everywhere except for her face.

They removed her fur coat and immediately saw that she was wearing nothing underneath, just a pair of slacks. The white flesh of her hips appeared neutral and dead in the light of the sodium vapor reflectors that lit up the freeway. Her zipper had already been pulled down by the time we crashed into the tree.

POSTFACE

Vernon Sullivans's first work provoked such a diverse array of reactions that I was encouraged to undertake, for the second work in the series of this young author, a second commentary as well. There is a certain advantage to this: there will be five or six more pages, which, as they say in the business, will add a bit of meat to the work itself. Anyway, it's not as bad idea discuss from time to time certain things with the readers in order to let them know that we do think about them.

Diverse reactions? Fine. Still, taken in their totality they permit us to come to a conclusion that is at once clear, unyielding, and implacable: with the exception of maybe a half dozen well-intentioned individuals, the critics have behaved like foolhardy dolts of the worst ilk.

The first issue concerns a passage from the original preface in which I made a remark about being able to earn a living (something that the publishers themselves had no trouble understanding). However, the above-mentioned critics decided rather blithely to attribute the paternity of this book me. This is the typical modus operandi of these villainous swine - simply stated, I am much too chaste and innocent to have written such things.

I hardly protested. After all, it was great publicity. Still, it's not true. Or maybe I should say it's more or less false. Concerning the details of the book, they made even more incredibly asinine remarks. Some were astonished by the number and abundance of American cars (obviously, they've never read Raymond Chandler). Others nit-picked over a variety of inanities upon which I will not dwell, because after all, it's vulgar to obsess over such stupidity. There was even an individual who claimed to be a black man from Martinique - his name alone is a half-Arab, half-archaistic insult to public decency – who affirmed that a Black man could never have written that book because he himself knows how Blacks live. Well, let's just say that this particular Black is about as qualified to comment upon his American brothers as a Chinese resident of San Francisco is capable of resolving the current upheavals in Shanghai. What's more, even if he has no desire to avenge his brother's death by sleeping with white women and reducing them rubble, that doesn't mean that there are not others who would do that very thing. But it gets worse.

Among all the critics, there are those who spat their green and gooey venom all over the first Sullivan book, and those who praised it to the hilt. These later elevated the book to a considerable status, and thus bestowed upon it a certain importance. It may in fact have some importance, but not the kind that they're talking about. Literally speaking, it is not a work that we should linger over obsessively.

Let's make this clear. I did a translation that is more or less written in French (not academic French, certainly, but respectable). Yet in my first preface, maddened by a nauseating concern for commercial success, I had taken the trouble to remind interested parties that a publisher (and they still want to ignore this) is essentially someone who's in the business of selling books.

And then they came and pounced, got right up into my face to tell me this was a filthy book, vile rubbish and all! It's not about Sullivan at all since it was Vian who translated it! Furthermore, it's not faithful to the details. It's not even faithful in the overall sense of the term. What's more, there are plenty of men who sleep with women and find pleasure in it. Stories about pederasts and lesbians…. It's disgusting! It's a return to barbarism, a disaster without precedent, the vapid imaginings of a desperate prankster, und so weiter!!!

Thus they continue to talk. About everything. Everything, that is, except the book itself. And now, poor little Vian is a plagiarist, an assassin, a pornographer, a miserable little shitstain, and, at the same time, an uncontrolled priapic beast, a Jean Legrand living the high life, the worst of the worst. So get lost, you lousy pig. You've been unmasked.

The story itself - the two hundred printed pages - they simply don't discuss. This isn't a phenomenon unique to this book. Generally speaking, it's how they operate. It's truly flabbergasting.

I'd be pleased as punch to talk about something else, but what we have here is an abscess that has to be driven to the surface, in hope that we can find a surgeon to eradicate, if possible, the hideous, multicephalous beast that is flourishing at its center.

You really are a bunch of sorry individuals, you so-called critics. Almost each and every one of you is as cretinous as Claude Morgan (which is no small indictment). When do you plan to start doing your job? When will you stop looking for yourselves in the books you read? A true reader deals with the book itself. So when will you stop asking yourself, at the very outset, if the author is Peruvian, schismatic, a member of the communist party, or a relative of André Malraux? When will you be able to speak of a book without limiting yourselves by making countless references to the author and all the details of the ins and outs of his or her life? Are you terrified of making a mistake? Because let me tell you, with all your precautions you simply end up making much bigger blunders. When will you admit that somebody can write for *Les Temps Moderns* without necessarily being an existentialist, or enjoy playing a practical joke from time to time? When will you simply permit us freedom?

But of course that won't happen. It's a word you're crossed out of your dictionary. Even worse, you've banished it from your already impoverished vocabulary.

Why do you talk about writers? You have no idea what one is. Still, when one knows nothing, one can always call upon one's imagination to cook something up. The problem is you don't have any imagination either, so you simply behave dishonestly. You deal only with what you understand. Take, for example, *I spit on your graves.*[1] There was really but one thing to say about this work, and the half-dozen critics cited above who happened to speak honestly about this book were able to honestly recognize its true nature: a good theme, well-developed, which could have been fine novel, even though it ran the risk of mediocre sales (the fault of the critics and publishers) which is a normal risk for any good novel, and which, when dealt with commercially, as it was, eventually became a popular book and a leisurely read that sold quite well. It is, after all, much less lurid than the Bible, and when I translated it I did so in an understated fashion as to not hurt future sales while at the same time showing enough of the raw truth so that the critics (I hoped) would be able to understand it. This was done for a simple reason: a steak is worth its weight in gold, and gold, after all, is quite expensive.

The result? The critics turned this book into a literary success (whether they trash a work or speak highly of it, when everyone is talks about a novel then it becomes a success). And other good books await their reviews. Still, in the end, when you so-called critics run up against a book you just don't understand, isn't it your job to tell us so? That would be the best thing you could do for the reader. But far from admitting that you've been surprised, you hide this fact. But surprise isn't even the right word: these works pass right over your head. I could cite twenty examples.

You critics are simply a bunch of dolts! If you want to talk about yourselves, go confess your sins at the Salvation Army. But when you deal with authors who actually have a unique vision and are trying to accomplish something, for God's sake just leave them the hell alone. It's high time you learn to be objective, please. You're treading on dangerous ground.

[1] Translation of *J'irai cracher sur vos tombes*, published by TamTam Books in 1998. (Translator's note).

BOOKS

TamTam Books Series:

Forthcoming:

For further informaiotn about these tiltles and authors:

www.tamtambooks.com